Copyright © 2024 by River Satine
All rights reserved.
No part of this publication may be reproduced, distributed, or transmitted in any form or by any means, including photocopying, recording, or other electronic or mechanical methods, without the prior written permission of the publisher, except as permitted by U.S. copyright law.
The story, all names, characters, and incidents portrayed in this production are fictitious. No identification with actual persons (living or deceased), places, buildings, and products is intended or should be inferred.
Book Cover by River Satine
Illustrations by River Satine

1st edition 2024

RIVER SATINE

THE MAIN CORPSE

COPYRIGHT © 2024 RIVER SATINE
ALL RIGHTS RESERVED

Chapter One

Hell's Kitchen

Eagerness turned to disdain the moment Valeria opened the doors. Though Val's had only been closed for a mere two months, the culinary world was stirred into a frenzy - anticipation growing for the new menu being launched. For Valeria, tonight was make or break - if she failed, her career would be finished - but if she succeeded, she'd cement Val's as one of the country's best restaurants.

The sounds of ironworkers filled the kitchen, as artisans of their craft plated their dishes and garnished their creations. Emorie, who had been closely by Valeria's side through the menu's creation, looked as though her arms would fall off at any given moment, as they moved swiftly and aggressively, stirring meals and moving pans from station to station. Two passionate dancers tangoed in the kitchen, matching the other's movements and sensing where they were and weren't needed. Both Valeria and her sous chef were of sound body and sound mind.

"Where is he?" an older, bald man questioned, wiping sweat from his forehead as he checked his watch. "The brat can't keep getting away with this! I cannot allow *him* to ruin the night for the rest of us." he complained.

"Bastard got the promotion and can't even step up to the plate. Typical." A younger man spoke, shaking his head back and forth. "How did you let this happen?" He turned to the older man.

"Don't you have tables to be served right now? Or are Gianna and Basil doing most of your work. Aren't you a man, Pierre?" the older man spoke with sternness, staring Pierre down.

"Harold! I think you're starting to get mad at the wrong guy! At least I'm here!" Pierre began. "And 'sides, I've gotten all my tickets, now all I can do is wait for the kitchen to catch up. Though, if I were in there…"

"But you're not, so get the hell back out on the floor and do your damn job asshole!" Harold barked, looking back at his watch. "Dammit!"

The backdoor of the kitchen slowly crept open, though the song and dance of the two culinary masters continued, disregarding the sudden interruption. A man with his hair in a bun, feathered earrings, and a black chef's coat walked in, as though he had no part in the storm treading through Valeria's kitchen.

"Mr. Hope, you are one hour and twenty-three minutes LATE! You were meant to start at 8:00 P.M sharp, not nearly 9:30! What do you have to say for yourself!?" Harold swooped in, grabbing the middle-aged chef by his ear.

"Geez old man, ya need to calm down! What's important is the fact I'm here, it's not *my* fault that my traumas were preventing me from showing up on time. My time awareness deficiency is a serious disability!"

"Just because you made up this ridiculous sham of an illness and put it on your job application as a disability, that does *not* validate it. Do you know just how important tonight is for Valeria? For *all of us*?" Harold emphasized.

"Has the VIP shown up yet?" the man asked.

"No." Harold shortly answered.

"So, why're you acting so anal about this? Are we even sure Redmond Thatcher is going to show up tonight?"

"Of course he will, do you not understand just how powerful of a chef Valeria Swifton is? For months, she has kept a tight lid on what she'd debut on her new menu, any food connoisseur who's in the know would show up here tonight!" Harold stressed.

"If ya say so, baldy." Casey winked before entering the battlefield, to which Harold shook his head in frustration, his face growing redder than the tomatoes on prep.

While the back of house had its share of problems, the front of house was in a much more synchronized state, so much so that there were no tables left with their orders untaken. Lead server Basil, who had been a part of the staff for the last six months, smiles, before taking a deep breath in and then out. She stood by the front podium, waiting for their VIP to arrive.

"How are things on the western front?" Pierre asked, as though he was begging for more work to do. "Whatcha got for me, cutie?"

"You can check on table four, if you really want to." Basil suggested, shrugging her head to the family of eight whose rambunctious adults were making more noise than the children.

"Yeah, you know, it's fine. I think you and Gigi got a hold of things out here." Pierre excused himself, but before he could walk back, a hand grabbed him by the shoulder, stopping him in place.

"Tonight's the most important night of our careers, and you're over here slacking off. Pierre, I thought I told you to stop hanging out with Casey. That good for nothing's habits are starting to rub off on you." a woman's sharp voice barked.

"Oh, didn't see you there, Gianna." Pierre began. "I don't know why you're mad at me; I wasn't the one that showed up nearly an hour and a half late."

"What?" The woman sternly questioned.

"...and drunk." he coughed.

"You've got to be kidding me! How the hell did he get that promotion?" Basil frustratingly questioned.

"Ya'll don't think Valeria's...you know...gulp gulp" Pierre started making a motion with his hand and mouth.

"Real mature, dumbass." Gianna rolled her eyes.

"When you two lovebirds are done, I need you to get your asses back to work!" Basil ordered, signaling back to table four.

"Pierre, go!" she commanded.

"Ugh, do I really?" he rolled his eyes, making his way.

"And you wonder why you got passed up." Gianna barked, before turning back to check on her tables.

  As the night proceeded, communication between the servers and kitchen were flowing smoothly, and before long, at 10:00 on the dot, an older man with a large coat and red scarf walked in. His brown hair was greased back with a marinade of hair gel, and his round glasses rested effortlessly on the tip of his nose. Behind him, a much younger man in a striped button-down shirt and a face full of freckles stood awkwardly.

"Mr. Thatcher!" Basil began, but before she could get another word in, she was interrupted.

"Redmond Thatcher! It's a pleasure to welcome you to Val's! My name is Harold Dunbar, the general manager of this fine establishment. How are you this evening?"

"Dunbar..." Redmond began. "Dunbar...Dunbar.." he repeated. "Oh, yes, I remember you quite well. You worked at the Maroni Factory restaurant ten years ago, did you not?" he chuckled. "How could I forget?"

"Basil!" the younger man greeted, interrupting Basil's focus on Redmond and Harold. "It's been a while, hasn't it?"

"Darren? Oh my god, how long has it been?" Basil jumped with surprise.

"Seven years fly by, don't they?" Darren chuckled.

"Has it really been that long? I can't believe it!" she smiled.

"How have you been?" she began. "What are you doing here?" she asked with enthusiasm.

"Red's my boss!" Darren gloated. "Well, more like a mentor, Red's taken me under his wing so that way I can become an expert critic."

"So you're going to be his successor? How fun!"

"Well, I don't know if successor is the right word, but nonetheless, it's a great learning experience." he affirmed. "So what're you doing here?" he asked with a curious amount of energy.

"Technically I'm running the floor, but *he* just so happens to love taking the spotlight. I think it's a generational thing."

"Oh, that's so great for you!" Darren nodded. "Though I thought once you graduated high school you would've gone to be the next master chef of the world."

"I gotta work my way up the ladder first, Darren. And besides, I'm fine with what I'm doing now." she pretended to smile with eagerness, though there was more resentment hidden behind the facade.

"Well, when we have more time to catch up, I hope you can tell me more about it!" Darren began.

As Basil and Darren continued their reunion, Redmond and Harold's conversation broke through.

"Well, Mr. Dunbar, it was a pleasure conversing with you after all this time. Hopefully, you don't completely disappoint and fail Valeria the same way you did the Maroni's!" he chuckled.

"Now, young miss, if you would kindly show us to our table." Redmond turned his attention to Basil.

"Tch-!" Before Harold could get a retort out, Basil met his gaze with an even scarier glare, one that could paralyze a monster, as if to say, "Hold your tongue, manager."

"Right this way." Basil smiled before ushering Redmond and Darren to their table.

While Basil and Harold were busy with their special guest, and Pierre tied up with the rough-housing family of adult children, Gianna felt that it was up to her to retain the normalcy of the restaurant. For her, this was the perfect time to prove to everyone that she was a serious contender for promotion, and to hopefully signal to Valeria that a mistake was made when promoting Casey.

"Excuse me, ma'am." a hand waved up, trying to get Gianna's attention. "I'm having A LOT OF TROUBLE WITH MY FOOD" the voice yelled, as though he were trying to get Redmond Thatcher's attention and not Gianna'."

"Great. It's *them*." she cringed, making her way to the nauseating table. She looked over at Pierre, who wore a devious grin on his face, as though he had known all the time that table four wasn't the most difficult enemy of the night.

"Motherfucker." she whispered to herself.

"Marcellus, to what do we owe the pleasure this evening?" She sarcastically asked.

"Oh good, it's the valley girl, here to save the day!" Marcellus chided. "Valeria's really letting this place go to the shits letting a gutter rat serve food to humans!" he mocked.

"Well, they say rats are attracted to shit, and here you are! So how can I help you tonight, Marshitus?" she clapped back.

"The nerve, I-" Marcellus was tripping over his own words, unable to gather himself in time for a response.

"And you-" Gianna turned her attention to the woman sitting across from Marcellus. "Turned to the dark side, Heather? It matches that soul of yours!"

"Now now, is that anyway to treat a guest? My my, I may have to lodge a formal complaint with Valeria, the magazine would be shocked to see how their star reporter gets treated. So much for fine dining." Heather complained.

"What do you want?" Gianna rolled her eyes, wanting more than anything to move to her next table.

"Is it true that there's more going on behind the scenes than meets the eye?" Heather poked.

"I've heard the same rumor as well; it may turn out to be quite the scandal!" Marcellus added on. "Would be an awful shame if Valeria got a taste of some bad press."

"Oh? Did she stop by your restaurant recently? She never mentioned..." Gianna clapped back. "Now, was there anything you actually needed, or should I just kick you out now?"

"My iced tea needs more sugar; would you be a darling and fetch me a fresh glass?" Heather interjected. "We can leave the pleasantries here, it's plain to see we'll get nowhere with you."

"Very well." Gianna smiled, before sharply turning around and heading to the back to fulfill Heather and the rest of Gianna's tables' request.

  The busyness of the restaurant made time fly for almost all of the staff. At around 11:00, tables began clearing and Alejandro made his way out to clean off what he could. "My time to shine! Alright!" he affirmed to himself, starting with a set of tables combined to look like one long table. There were stains on the tablecloth, with glasses tilted over and spills everywhere. There were crumbs all over the floor and it looked as though someone had been whisked away to the land of Oz.

"What ever happened to manners? Etiquette, even…?" Alejandro asked himself, losing all his hope in humanity.

"Hey, Al, how's it going?" Pierre asked, walking up behind Alejandro.

"Just trying to get this place cleared, I really don't wanna have to stay overnight, Pierre." he responded.

"Well, mister tight ass, I just swung by to let you know that the crew is gonna head out back soon for a smoke. His royal highness demands the space for himself for the duration of his review."

"Oh, for real? That doesn't really make much sense." Alejandro was puzzled.

"Redmond Thatcher does more than taste food, he critiques the quality of the staff, the restaurant itself, and the equipment we use - his opinion in the culinary world is no joke!" Pierre answered fanatically.

"Sounds like you got a hard on for him, heh." Alejandro jokes.

"S-shut up, bro!" Pierre gently punches Alejandro's arm. "You can take back what you have now and finish the rest later, Valeria's orders." Pierre signaled for the back and Alejandro followed behind closely.

"Make sure everything is turned off before we head out, the floor has been cleared and now Mr. Thatcher moves onto the second stage of his review process." Harold began lecturing. "Valeria and Emorie have already headed out back and are awaiting you all."

Basil and Gianna, who were chatting through his rambling, headed directly out, laughing over the strange customer interactions they had through the night.

"Marshitus, really?" Basil giggled.

"Yeah, you should've seen his sorry ass!" Gianna chuckled.

"Wanna go see if he's off at his own shithole having a hissy fit?

"Ladies, glad to see you're having a good time on a night as consequential as this!" Harold chided.

"Lay off them old man." Casey mocked, running into the middle of Alejandro and Pierre. "The night's nearly over, can't you loosen that tight asshole of yours?"

"Mr. Hope, I hope you realize that your etiquette is not-"

"..any of your concern, geezer! Don't you realize I'm higher on the totem pole than you are? You're old news!"

Pierre coughed before interjecting. "I heard if anyone would be a letdown, it would've been you, Harry."

"Pierre!"

"Something about Maro-"

"Pierre! Cease this at once!" Harold's face once again grew red from frustration, as he stomped his foot on the ground, turned, and then proceeded to march out like a soldier to war.

"I knew I liked ya!" Casey gave Pierre a high five, the both of them heading off to the convenience store across the street for a pack of cigarettes.

Alejandro grew quiet as he slowly became the third wheel in the duo that was Casey and Pierre, both of whom had a strong bond with the other. Once outside, Alejandro trailed off and stood next to Redmond's assistant, who had remained with the staff,

"Oh, are you not assisting with the inspection?" Alejandro asked Darren, who turned over and smiled.

"Normally yes, but tonight he dismissed me and said this review had to be done privately." Darren replied.

"Really? How come?"

"A personal request from Valeria, as far as I understand. That's why I assume she's inside with Red, maybe wanting to talk about something." Darren suggested.

"Have ya seen Em?" Alejandro asked.

"The sous chef? No, not recently. Everyone seems to have gone off to do their own thing while Red does his thing, so I'm sure they'll all be back soon. Why? Ya got the softs for her?" Darren teased.

"N-no, there were just a few questions I wanted to ask, that's all! Honest!" Alejandro answered nervously.

"And I totally believe you dude!" Darren jokingly reassured Alejandro. "If you want to talk with her so badly, why don't we walk around and see if we can find her?" he suggested, to which Alejandro nodded in agreement.

***

While the staff of Val's were out of his hair, Redmond found this time to be the perfect opportunity to engage in the second phase of his review. Thatcher was no stranger to the culture of fine dining, it's a field he's known all too well since birth. For him, the food of a restaurant can only be as good as those who make it, those who serve it, and the place in which it's created.

The night had been full of surprises, running into a few surprises faces he did not expect to meet. For starters, Redmond was a bit shocked that Valeria chose to recuse herself from greeting him, as she had personally invited him to the grand opening.

"It appears that not even the illustrious Valeria Swifton can maintain the perfect illusion." he complained, making his way to the kitchen with his pen and notepad in hand.

The kitchen itself was surprisingly hot, as though the temperature had been turned to triple digits. Redmond found himself wiping off sweat from his forehead. Looking around the kitchen, Redmond was in a state of alert, as it looked as though the entire kitchen was still in use. There were packs of sugar all over the floor, wet spots splattered all around, and every stovetop, grill, and fryer had been turned on to the highest setting.

"Leaving dangerous equipment unattended? Tsk. Tsk. Very messy." he shook his head, jotting a few notes down on his paper. "I cannot believe Valeria Swifton would allow this to happen! I am truly appalled by the pig!"

When Redmond looked up, finally looking around at more than just the state of affairs in the kitchen, he noticed a figure coated in black standing in front of the stove, with their hands on the pot, Redmond not able to see exactly what they were doing. There were spots of sugar alongside the counter where the figure stood.

"You there!" he pointed to the person. "Weren't you told to leave this vicinity? What is the meaning of all this? Don't you know anything about kitchen safety, how could you just-" before Redmond could finish scolding them, the individual quickly turned around, boiling pot in hand, wearing a burnt and tethered mask that looked like a face from nightmares. The front of the burnt coat was decorated with spikes and chains. The masked figure aggressively dumped the boiling water over Redmond's face, severely burning him.

"Oh my god! Oh my god! What the hell!?" Redmond shrieked, with his vision turning black. Redmond covered his face with his hands as skin just continued to melt off. He began taking steps back. "Help! Somebody!!!" he screamed in pain, with his voice cutting out. The figure took another pan still on the stove and dumped it all over Redmond. In immense pain, Redmond kept his hand over his face, but the more he tried to get ahold of it, the more it came off. The killer slammed the now empty pot over Redmond's head, knocking him back, to which he tripped on a wet spot and his head fell against the edge of a counter, a faint crack being heard. They took a bag of ice from the freezer and dumped it into the fryers - the sound of the oil filling the room and over pouring onto the floors.

    At the exit, the killer turned to look at the catastrophe in front of them, taking a match from their pocket, sparking it and throwing it down onto the kitchen floors, the flame rapidly growing and spreading. They quickly turned back and fled the scene, the sounds of a burning, explosive crime scene overtaking the rest of the street.

***

The violence of the flames raging across Val's reunited those who had gone off to wait for the completion of Redmond's review. The nine who remained on the outside stood in shock and horror over the blazing tremors of the fire.

"M-my restaurant!" Valeria screamed. "How could this happen?" she cried.

"What the hell happened here!?" Harold aggressively asked, looking around. "Did I not say to turn everything off!?"

"Not the time, Harold." Basil barely muttered, her hands covering her mouth.

"Where's Redmond!?" Darren nervously questioned, running up close to the flames. Basil and Alejandro ran up to him and held him back, as he kept trying to push through. "GUYS, WHAT HAPPENED TO REDMOND?" he screamed, his cries silenced out by the sounds of sirens.

Chapter Two

Suddenly, Last Summer

Basil found herself looking back at the silhouette she saw when the fire had burned down Val's. A year later, and the hauntingly grim memory left her somewhat paranoid. She wondered, though for a brief moment, if what she had seen was a figment of her imagination, or a real legitimate person. When the fire was put out, the charred corpse of Redmond Thatcher had discovered - a brutal end to the future hopes of not only Val, but also Basil and the rest of the staff. As Basil stared out the window ahead of her, a voice snapped her back to reality.

"Hey? Hello? Excuse me!" a woman's voice shouted, snapping her fingers over Basil's face. "I'd like to place my order!" she demanded.

"Oh, well, uh-" Basil jumped, a little startled over the rude customer. "What can I get started for you?" she asked with a smile.

When she wasn't dealing with the avalanche of customers that would tumble down on her, Basil would prepare muffins and other baked goods in the back - a painstakingly tedious job that she was never able to quite complete. Every time she would go back and begin the process, a customer would materialize from what seemed to be thin air. Tired of this relentless back and forth, Basil decided to conduct an experiment. For the next hour, Basil remained at the register, anticipating that she'd catch the volley of customers. However, for the entirety of that hour, not a single customer walked in. Composed, and figuring she'd be safe to resume her baking activities, Basil began to head towards the back. As she began pouring out some flour from the bin, the bell at the entrance rang, and a "Hello" from a customer could be heard.

Running a bakery was not the life she had anticipated, however Basil counted herself as fortunate that her parents were looking to retire and leave her the family business. Rows of colorful and delectable sweets lined up the shelves and fridges, from parfaits with glazed berries, to sugar frosted donuts encrusted with pieces of bacon. The smell of freshly baked treats leaving the oven consumed the nostrils of anyone who walked in. Basil prided herself on the cozy aesthetic that she had meticulously crafted.

There was a part of her that felt remorseful, however, a distinct pressure of pain and irritation that plagued the rather sweet nature of her bakery. It had been seven months since she had last talked to any of the crew from Val's, and as invested as she was, Basil felt as if she had neglected to check in on her old friends. She wondered if they were doing alright, if they had managed to find their footing elsewhere in the culinary world as she had.

Nearing the end of her shift, Basil began her closing procedures and prepared to leave exactly at five, given the light foot traffic throughout the day. With a few minutes to go, a sudden phone call ruined the tranquility Basil had going. "If this is a catering order..." she began. "...after I *just* finished."

Letting out a heavy sigh, she remorsefully answered the phone.

"Talbot's Treats, Basil speaking. How may I help you this evening?" she greeted, smiling with a slight twitch.

"It sounds like your customer service voice has gotten sloppy, kid." the voice of a familiar woman teased.

"V-Valeria!?" Basil jumped back, slightly shaking in remembrance of their last interaction with the other.

"We've gotten casual now, haven't we?" she chuckled. "I've seen your work over social media the past few months, and I must say that I am really impressed by your work ethic."

"Thanks!" Basil sharply replied.

"There's no need for you to respond with such trepidation, Basil." Valeria began. "I call bearing good news and hopefully good opportunities."

Basil took a moment to collect her thoughts. "Opportunities?" she said to herself.

"You there, kid?" Valeria shouted through the phone.

"Uh, yeah! What's the news?" Basil questioned

"Well, I know it's been quite a long time since we last spoke, and I know that all of us didn't really end off on a good note, but I'm here with an offer." Valeria explained.

"And what would that be, Valeria?"

"A position, *your* position, at my new restaurant I'm launching within the next week. I spoke with Emorie and the rest of the team, and they've all agreed to come back. But without you, my new restaurant will be incomplete."

"Really?"

"Of course, without you, the whole machine would fall apart entirely. You expertly handle any and all customer complaints, as well as any internal arguments that may arise. You're my asset." Valeria proudly complimented her.

"When would I need to give you my answer?"

"Heh" Valeria quietly laughed. "I'm afraid it would have to be immediately, Basil."

The angel and devil on her shoulder weighed the options of staying in Maplewood or returning to Amber Creek. If she were to go back, the ghosts of the past year would return to haunt her in full force. And if she stayed behind, Basil would continue to live a life of blissful passivity, fading into the background of culinary excellence. But at the same time, she wouldn't have to deal with the pressures and pain that are inflicted by Valeria and the rest of the industry.

"Do I have your answer?" Valeria prodded.

"I have my answer." Basil confirmed, remaining unsure and hesitant about whether or not she was making the correct decision.

***

A vulgar scent of cigarettes and liquor fumigated the tightly knit 700 square foot apartment. There were wrappers and magazines littered on nearly every footage of the floor. The sound of an obnoxious snore, the same kind that you'd hear from a sleeping giant slumbering in the depths of a cave echoed across the apartment.

Pierre was awoken by a loud knock on his door, nearly falling backwards into the recliner he had sunken himself into. The knocking got louder and faster, as Pierre drunkenly stumbled his way like a zombie to the front door.

"Pierre, get your lazy, good for nothing ass out here right this fucking instant! I will SWAT this place in the next FIVE minutes if I don't see you!" A woman's voice furiously roared.
"Damn, hold your horses babe!" Pierre opened the door to see an angered Gianna greet him with a slap on the face.
"Did I say you could call me babe, you dipshit!?" she mocked. She sniffed the air. "Are you *drunk*? Today, of all days, are you serious!? It's 10 in the morning!" she scolded with concern. "Honestly, what am I gonna do with ya?" Gianna rolled her eyes and helped to carry Pierre back into his chair before he could fall over.

    Despite no longer dating, Giana still felt as though she had an obligation to fulfill - one to help her ex-boyfriend from going off the edge. There was a part of her that resented Pierre for how far he had fallen, though in a way, she understood his pain. Most days, Pierre would either sit in bed or on his recliner, and usually fade into a drunken slumber for more than half of the day. When Valeria called Gianna specifically to offer her and Pierre their old positions back, Gianna felt that maybe this would be the key to breaking the curse, and to return Pierre back to his former self.

"Pierre!" she clapped. "Look at me!" she demanded, waving her palm in front of his face.

"Gigi?" he began. "What're you doing here?" Pierre rubbed his left cheek, mouthing "shit" from the pain of Gianna's earlier slap.

"You let me in- ugh never mind...today's the day we head back to Val's." Gianna explained. "...Remember?"

"Oh! Yeah!" Pierre slowly nodded.

    Pierre, even though he looked like he was as drunk as a sailor, pretended to be buzzed. He was fully aware of what day it was, but he didn't care, it made no difference to him. Over the course of the year, the more he drank, the less alcohol affected him. It had gotten to the point where vodka became the new water. Fully aware of the consequences, Pierre found himself unable to stop, for when he was fully sober - memories of that day one year ago would consume his every thought. Pierre rubbed his ankle before twitching a little from the pain, reflecting on what had happened the night Val's burned down. He rubbed his eyes together before stretching and shaking. With a loud yawn, he got up to go and take a shower, limping as he took each step. Gianna, letting out a sigh of concern, helped walk Pierre and prepare him for what laid before them.

***

Unsure of where things were heading, Basil prepared for what she felt would be a brutal war. When she drove back into Amber Creek, a rush of nostalgia overcame her. One part of her was excited over the prospects of reuniting with Gianna and the rest of her coworkers, however the other was shrouded in doubt - paranoid that something bad was about to happen. Consumed by her thoughts, Basil pulled over underneath a tree with vibrant, green leaves. She took a moment to collect herself before proceeding forward.

Despite being away for over a year, most of Amber Creek remained the same - something she quite enjoyed about the town. Basil hated change and cringed at the thought of a town no longer the same - wanting more sameness and less newness. Maplewood had been a challenge for her, the terrain and energy being on a completely different level from that which she was typically used to. There was a part of Amber Creek that was no longer the same - at least for Basil. Whenever she looks around at the town, all she can feel is the sting of failure. The place where her dreams were burned to cinders.

From what she can remember, Val's was an extravagant fine dining establishment to fit at most twenty-five people. Leaves covered most of the outer walls greeting the streets, with lights flickering from the windows looking into the restaurant. The inside was grand and had dark red walls with a black finish, and the floors were checkered with black marble and white marble. Basil had been exceptionally proud to work under Valeria Swifton at Val's, not only for the pride in where she worked, but also for the service she performed. It's because of this that Basil decided to return to Amber's Creek to work under Val, it gave her a chance to return to the sameness she remembered so well.

When Basil stepped out of her car to the front steps of Valeria's new restaurant, she heard a slam, and all she could smell was smoke. The scent overtook her nostrils, almost to the point of her passing out. The restaurant in front of her was covered in a violent red flame, to which Basil nearly screamed in horror. However, after one more sniff of the air, and a combustion of rapid-fire winking, Basil realized there was no smoke at all. Fully looking to the front of the new restaurant, she was floored by the transformation Val's had undergone. In the same space where the former culinary stronghold once stood, lay a new restaurant that looks larger, grander, and even more expensive than the one before. The new building stood taller than its predecessor - a massive structure that shadowed over the restaurant across the street, Amore, Val's rival restaurant ran by the persnickety Marcellus Derdrew.

Parked near the end of the parking lot was a red sedan with heavily tinted windows. Basil found this to be strange, as it was a car she was unfamiliar with. Scattered across the parking lot were the cars of her old coworkers - a sight she remembered very well. The sound of feet shuffling from behind Basil alerted her to the fact that there was someone else hiding from her in the parking lot. She turned around as she heard the shuffling immediately cease, however there was nobody in sight. When she turned around, she could see nothing. The closer to the restaurant she got, the louder the other footsteps got, and as she stopped and turned to catch whoever it was, she jumped back with alertness. The woman following had bumped against Basil and was pushed back.

"My my." the woman commented, brushing herself off, picking up her red beret that had fallen on the floor. "You truly must watch your surroundings more carefully, Ms. Talbot." she said, looking up at Basil.

"Who the hell are you? Better yet why are you just lurking in a parking lot in the middle of the day?" Basil questioned.

"My name is Heather Madden." she smiled, taking out a business card and handing it to Basil. The business card read "Heather Madden: Journalist / Starr Magazine".

"A journalist, really?"

"Yes yes, I'm a culinary reporter for Starr Magazine, and I have quite the splendid history with this establishment." she nodded. "I'm here on the rumor that Valeria is reopening a new restaurant at this location."

"Rumor?" Basil's face turned sour. "I don't understand what you mean by rumor, there's a sign as you enter the parking lot that says "Val's", with a wrap that says, "Coming Soon" across it." she pointed out. What's your angle, Heather?"

"Well, I, uh…You see-" Heather got surprisingly flustered, but before she could make out an excuse, another voice thwarted her.

"The hell are you doing here, Heather?" a familiarly aggressive voice asked. "Do I need to get the spray bottle?" she sarcastically prowled.

"Why Gianna, there's no need for such hostility. After all this time, must we still act on such sour emotions?" she asked with a faux sound of concern.

"Please, the only thing sour here is Marcellus' rotten cooking!" Gianna roared.

"Hey!" a man's voice defensively shouted, standing up from behind the car.

"Where there's tweedle dumb, dumber is always nearby!" Gianna barked, turning to Marcellus. "Get outta here before I start getting really angry!"

With an "eep" and an "ack", Marcellus and Heather retreated back across the street to Amore, cursing Gianna off in the process.

"Basil! It's good to see ya!" Gianna smiled before hugging Basil. "I can't believe how long it's been, I'm so happy to see you again!" Basil smiled. Though, she questioned Gianna's warmth, having expected a much colder reaction.

"So, I see ya got the call too, huh?" Gianna asked. "She called Pierre and I around a day or two ago, and we couldn't say no!"

"Yeah, it was the same for me. How are you? How's Pierre doing?" Basil enthusiastically asked, met with a change in tone and expression from Gianna.

"We've been doing okay." she said plainly. "Anyways, let's get you inside, everyone else is here as well!"

The interior of Val's had changed drastically from how Basil had remembered it. This came as no surprise to her considering the extent of the damage. But as far as she was concerned, the new look was a steadfast improvement from the one before. The roof was clear to let the sunshine through, giving anyone on the inside a pleasant view of the sky above. There were lights dimly lit around the restaurant which looked as though it could feed at least a hundred people. The walls were a shade of grassy green, with a light brown finish, and the floors were refined with teakwood, giving the restaurant a very comforting, cozy, and nature-like vibe. Seated at the long, extended table at the center of the restaurant were the staff members of Val's.

"Basil! Very good!" a familiar old bald man said approvingly.

"Harold! I'm glad you're here!" Basil smiled at the man who mentored her straight out of culinary school.

"Now how come I didn't receive such a fond greeting when I showed up?" A middle-aged man with long hair and a feather earring complained.

"Respect is earned, not given, boy. And the only thing you've earned from me is a foot up your ass!" Harold barked.

"Boys! Aren't you here to act like men? Get a hold of yourselves!" a young, blonde-haired woman scolded, before turning to Basil. "It's good to see you, Basil."

"Nice seeing you again too, Emorie." Basil greeted, before heading to sit at the spot next to Gianna. "And Casey, maybe if you showed a little more respect, Harold would give you some of his. Just saying." she chuckled to a sighing Casey.

To the right of Gianna sat Pierre, who barely gave Basil as much as a glance when she arrived. Across from Pierre and next to Emorie and Harold was Alejandro, the busser who Basil had never really gotten close to in all the time they worked together, but who was also fairly close with Emorie. Basil was a little surprised that Emorie would return to work under Valeria, considering Emorie had been making quite the name in the culinary world over the past year. Also seated next to Harold, much to both their dismay, was Casey - who was doing everything but sitting still. Despite the chaos, Basil felt more at peace, glad that there were still some things in Amber Creek that hadn't changed.

Interrupting the bantering was a loud clap, followed by the immediate silence of the entire staff, similar to a mother gathering her children. Walking down the stairs was a crimson-haired beauty wearing a black chef's coat with a red lining. The sound of her shoes against the floor echoed throughout the silent tomb. She smiled before greeting her staff.

"It's so grand that we have all made it back here!" she greeted with a smooth, velvety voice - which sounded much nicer than it did when Basil heard it on the phone. "I trust we've all been well?" she asked to a response of approving nods.

Basil was in awe of Valeria's overwhelmingly powerful presence, and the respect that radiated from staff member to chef.

"As I told you all on the phone, I plan on reopening Val's within the next week. And as you've all probably seen from our nosey neighbors, all eyes will be on us." she spoke. "I have crafted a new menu, carefully catered to meet the needs and desires of all food connoisseurs." she proudly announced, to the excitement of her staff. Emorie, however, Basil noticed, reacted a little less positively than the rest. "Over the course of this week, leading up to the reopening, I will keep a watchful eye on all of your behavior and prowess during and out of training. At the end of the week, I will choose one of you to work alongside Emorie and myself.

"What!?" Casey coughed. "What about me?"

"What about you Casey, I really don't think you're in any position to complain about being here." she chided.

"We'll see about that." he mumbled to himself.

"Heh. Looks like the pretty boy won't get his way." Pierre chuckled before being nudged by Gianna, who wanted him to remain quiet.

    Basil found this to be a chance to rekindle her dream, a chance to once again find herself back in the culinary hall of fame. It was as though the universe was guiding her on the right path, and that pretty soon, the fruits of her labor would finally flourish.

"Continuing on." Valeria began again. "I understand many of us may still have reservations - worries and doubts concerning the events of the past year." she said to the grim reactions of the staff, who looked remorseful. "It was very difficult for us to lose my restaurant, believe me I know better than most about this, however we must tread forward! Though Redmond fell to the flames, the same does not need to be for us. We must rise from the ashes to become the master chef's we were all born to be! Like the phoenixes we are!" she proudly proclaimed.

"I knew I could put my faith in you once more. Let's win, shall we?" Harold proudly declared.

"I have a good feeling about this, don't you?" Alejandro said to a mild tempered Emorie.

"Pierre? Don't you think this is great!? We have a shot again!"

"Hell yeah we do!" Pierre enthusiastically responded to Gianna, with a fire lit under his eyes.

"Isn't this wonderful?" Valeria turned to Basil as the rest celebrated. "I'm sincerely happy, for all of you!" she cheered.

    Suddenly, last summer began to feel like nothing more than a bad dream for Basil, who was ready to move forward.

Chapter Three

Since You've Been Gone

It felt kind of fitting for Pierre - to have a mixed salad of emotions, different ingredients ranging from happy to excited to bitter and remorseful. The past year had felt like a never-ending nightmare that he couldn't escape from, the spark that fueled his fire having been extinguished. Looking back to when Casey had initially been promoted, neither he nor the rest of the staff could figure out Valeria's logic. He hated Casey for the special treatment he'd been given, it was unfair to people like Pierre, who had devoted his entire life to cooking only to be chalked up as waiter. A pain jolted through Pierre's left ankle as he sat at the table, Valeria just finishing her grand speech. "This is great." he thought to himself, until he took a quick glance at Basil, with feelings of resentment stirring inside. He noticed the look of concern Gianna had on her face, noticing his distasteful stare. "Why did *she* have to come back?" he pondered, staring off into space.

"Earth to Pierre." Gianna snapped her fingers to regain his attention.

"Yeah? What is it?" Pierre carelessly responded.

Pierre never understood why Gianna had stuck with him through this time, especially with how he had treated her and been treating himself. "She deserves better." he figured, staring at Basil.

"We're gonna check out the new kitchen setup, loverboy. Care to join the rest of us in the land of sobriety?" Casey sarcastically commented.

"I'm surprised you even know what a kitchen is, Casey. Considering you do more complaining than you do cooking." Pierre dryly responded.

"Now children, please remember who's paying attention." Emorie interrupted, noting the glare from Valeria's direction.

"Yeah. Sorry." Pierre said.

"Yeah. Sorry" Casey said mockingly. "Kiss ass." he muttered into Pierre's ear.

"Listen here motherfu-"

"Pierre! Let's get going!" Gianna cut him off,

"I need a drink." Pierre complained.

"Like hell you do, asshole." Gianna scolded.

While the rest of the staff were talking, Pierre was off in his own world, only remaining semi aware of his surroundings - most of his attention being lost in a maze of his own thoughts. "There's no way I have a shot anymore." he sighed to himself, limping his way to the kitchen.

Pierre was amazed by the state-of-the-art kitchen Valeria had managed to put together, a design she put into effect herself. There were even more stovetops and fryers than there were in the old restaurant, with mandolin slicers, knives, and other necessary kitchen tools properly placed all around. "Is that what I think it is?" Alejandro pointed out, speedily walking to the back sinks.

"Very astute observation, Alejandro". Valeria commented. "I recall how time-consuming dishes took once we closed, and I figured keeping up with the times would make things easier for all of us." she smiled.

"Our very own hobart, wow." his eyes gleamed with excitement.

Pierre didn't understand the excitement from Alejandro, as a dishwasher was just a dishwasher, there was nothing particularly special about it - to Pierre at the very least. He looked at the mandolin slicer that was on one of the equipment shelves, reflecting back on his time trying to use one in the past.

"You cut yourself a couple of times with this bad boy, didn't you?" Basil teased, standing next to Pierre, trying to start a conversation with him.

"Wow, talk about a clutz. Personally, I would *never* let that happen." Casey poked into the conversation.

"Thanks for bringing that up, Basil, really." Pierre complained, before walking off to be near Gianna and Harold, who were looking into the massive walk-in freezer.

"What a massive freezer." Gianna commented,

"Truly magnificent." Harold nodded. "I remember just how compact the old one was, always making food storage such a tedious task."

"It really makes you appreciate what you have, doesn't it?" Gianna replied.

"Indeed." Harold confirmed. "You never know just how good you have something, until you lose it entirely."

"Tch." Pierre shook his head.

"Is something the matter, Mr. Whitlock?" Harold questioned.

"No." there was a slight pause. "I just need a minute." Pierre assured Harold and Gianna, before stepping out to the back for a quick smoke.

There were too many changes going on around him, and Pierre found himself frustrated by the rate at which people moved on. "Why hasn't anybody talked about it!?" he said to himself in frustration, punching the dumpster. "Something new and shiny, and all of a sudden, the world is such a beautiful place. Disgusting." he said with frustration. "Ugh. Where's a drink when you need one?" he complained.

"Isn't it too early to be drinking?" Basil said, cautiously walking closer to Pierre.

"What's it to you?" he snapped, Basil being taken aback.

"Pierre..." Basil's voice trailed off.

"Oh? I'm sorry, did you care?"

"You know I do."

"Could've fooled me!" Pierre barked. "Did you really think you could leave this shithole for a year and the welcome wagon would be here waiting with open arms? You're a lot dumber than I remembered!"

"Look, I'm sorry that I just got up and left so abruptly but I..."

"But what, Basil? But *what*? At the end of the day, you left, and it's all your fault that-" Pierre stopped himself before he could say anything further.

"You're not the only one who was dealing with shit, Pierre! I'm sorry I didn't prioritize your health over mine! I was wrong!"

"Oh, don't pull that shit with me, you know I hate it."

"What shit are you talking about!?"

"That self-sacrificing bullshit you pull. You always do shit to hurt others and then play the martyr. It's so fucking tiring." Pierre yelled.

"I regret not staying to help you and Gianna-"

"There you go!" he complained. "Why'd you have to say her name too?" he complained to himself. "You can go and fuck off with those regrets of yours, I really don't give one shit, Basil."

"Pierre..." Basil stuttered, her voice shaking. She stopped to regain her composure before continuing on. "Well at least I was able to move the fuck on." she began. "What have you done, other than berate women and blame others for your problem? Huh? Start a glass bottle collection? Yeah, I could smell it the moment I walked in." Basil reprimanded. "I wanted to apologize and make amends with you, truly, but you've shown me that there's absolutely nothing worth feeling sorry over, asshole." she shouted. "Now do your fucking job and don't let Valeria and the rest of us down!" she reprimanded, turning to walk away, bumping into Gianna, who had listened in on their conversation. "Sorry. I guess I shouldn't have come back." she wiped a tear away before returning to the kitchen.

"Basil, no-" Basil was already gone before Gianna could say anything back. "Are you happy with yourself, you giant piece of shit?" Gianna turned her attention to Pierre, who was turned away from her smoking his cigarette.

"So, you're gonna side with that bitch too, huh?"

"Excuse you? Pierre, I'm going to pretend you didn't just say that. What the hell is wrong with you?"

"What the hell is wrong with me? What the hell is wrong with her? With you!?" he said in disgust. "All you do is talk like nothing happened, it's total BS!"

"It's called moving on, dipshit! We can't be consumed by the past for the rest of our lives! You know this! What happened last year was horrible, truly, but there was nothing we could've done, it was a huge accident!"

"Are you even sure about that? How can you say something with such certainty?" Piere said with doubt.

"Because just like the rest of us, I can't speculate on the what ifs. For my own sake, I have to move forward, we all do!"

"Oh fuck off wth that nonsense. Why are you even siding with her? What about *me*!?"

Gianna took a step back and raised her eyebrows in disgust.

"Are you being for real right now, seriously?"

"Yeah, I am Gigi, what about me huh? What about my side, my thoughts, my feelings!? Huh!?" he pushed.

"I've been with you every step of the goddamn way since the accident, since your ankle! What have I been to you this last year? Was I just your fucking maid or was I a friend who was seriously concerned about your wellbeing, your addiction!"

"If you were really my friend you wouldn't have broken up with me. You would've sided with me just now."

"Oh my god you're completely mental, Pierre!" Gianna said with frustration. "It's like talking to a fucking brick wall."

"Well, if talking to me is such a bother, then you can just leave me the hell alone, I don't need you anyways.

"...Wow..." Gianna said with an exasperated gasp. "We're over, for good." she shook her head in anger.

"Then what are you still doing here?" Pierre questioned, shrugging her off with a motion of his arm. "If you're gonna stay here like an annoying gnat the least you could do is get me a drink." He turned to see if she was still there, but Gianna walked back inside before he had finished his last remark. Pierre remained alone and isolated in the back alleyway, shaking his head and lighting a new cigarette.

***

Despite the brightness of the dining room, a looming darkness hung over Val's. Basil was completely taken aback by the argument with Pierre, but there was a part of her that understood the pain which he was coming from. There was a part of her that felt as though she deserved the accosting she received, but at the same time, it felt unfair. After the fire, there was an unspoken rule that the staff had agreed to nonverbally - to just not bring up that night. Basil felt that it would be for the better - that if the past had been brought back up it would only lead to more harm, more danger than what was needed. She sat at a table on the main floor, teary-eyed, staring out the window and reflecting on the year that had passed. Basil wanted to make amends, but now it felt that she would never get the chance to redeem herself in the eyes of her former friends. "If Pierre thinks so little of me...what about the others?" she pondered.

"There she is. I was wondering where you ran off to, Basil." Harold joyfully commented, walking up behind Basil. When she turned to look at him, still with tears falling from her face,

Harold's expression changed from jolly to sympathetic. "What on earth happened to you?" he asked with concern.

"The consequences of my own actions." she began. "Don't worry, it's nothing." she tried to reassure him.

"Nonsense. Have you forgotten just how far back we go? I could never leave my former student, no, my friend, in such a state of distress." he stubbornly responded, taking the seat across from Basil. "Now let's discuss, shall we?"

Basil knew better, she knew that Harold, despite his many flaws, would never leave someone he cared about alone. There was a part of her that felt grateful to have someone as caring as him on her side, but another part of her felt guilty, dragging him into her personal mess.

"Harold, do you think there's a place for me here, after all this time?" she asked, looking him in the eyes.

"Why of course there is, my young prodigy, you're the future of cooking after all." he assured her. "Is that why you're in such a frenzy? Are you having a wave of self-doubt?"

"More or less. After my conversation with Pierre, I'm not sure if I made the correct move returning to Amber Creek."

"Mr. Whitlock? What did that man say to you that got you so ruffled?"

"Nothing I haven't thought of myself." she shrugged.

"Pay him no mind, I do not believe he is in the proper headspace to be having any serious form of conversation at the moment." Harold began, "I could tell the moment he walked in that there was something off." he continued, with a hint of disappointment. "But I think that's the case for the majority of us here."

"What do you mean?

"Well, to be frank, I think Mr. Thatcher's death and the fire took a heavy toll on us all. But we all handle things differently from each other. I planned on simply retiring after that night, not thinking I could ever step foot in the kitchen. There's no correct way of grieving or dealing with trauma." he started. "But a chance to work with you and Valeria once more had changed all that."

"But I left you all, without hesitation."

"And that's your right, Basil. You don't owe us any explanation. Now, I'll admit I was a tad bit hurt by your decision, but I fully understood and respected it. That goes for the rest of us as well, we all made the conscious choice to stay in town while you decided to leave and move on. But look at you, running a very successful bakery in Maplewood!"

"I don't know if successful is the word I'd use, and my parents gave me the business, it's not like I earned it."

"Nonsense! I highly doubt they would have entrusted you with a highly respectable business if they felt you weren't ready for it." Harold nodded. "And aside from that, I made a secret shipment order for a dozen of your muffins a few months back, and pride only begins to describe what I felt when tasting your delicious baked goods." he complimented.

"You did?" Basil questioned.

"But of course, what kind of teacher would I be if I did not support the ventures of my students? Naturally, I used an alias however - I didn't want you to overreact and go out of your way to do something more just because I ordered from you." he chuckled. "By the way, those glazed pumpkin spice muffins are absolutely heavenly."

"Harold..." Basil began, wiping the last of her tears from her face.

"Never doubt the decisions you make to better yourself, Basil. I mean it. Stand behind your decisions and don't ever falter - regardless of what some miserable drunk might say." he smiled.
"Thank you, I don't know if I could've made it this far without your support." Basil said with gratitude.
"He's a wise man, Basil. You'd be smart to trust in his words." Emorie spoke, interrupting the conversation and walking into the dining room.
"Emorie?" Basil questioned.
"In a way, I'm jealous of your courage, and your ability to trudge past your traumas. Not all of us have that strength." Emorie agreed with Harold. "After all, out of the entire staff here, I find you to be my greatest adversary, someone I can trust to push me past my limits." she spoke.
"I...I really don't know what to say."
"Well, instead of saying something, you can just stay with us and work towards that kitchen spot you deserve." Valeria chimed in, standing next to Emorie. "Didn't I tell you over the phone just how essential you were to the team, Basil?"
"Yeah...when I first started here you were the one who uplifted me the most, giving me tips and tricks to do my job better."

Alejandro said, appearing from the kitchen. "We need you!" he smiled.

"Well, Basil? Do you see now just how important you are? You have no reason to doubt you being here, no reason to fear the rest of us resenting you for moving forward." Harold nodded, looking at the staff and then back to Basil.

"You're right." she began. "Thank you, all of you. I don't know what I'd do if you weren't here." she smiled with joy.

It was at this moment that the doubts that had clouded Basil's mind had cleared away, and the sun shining through the glass ceiling began shining into Basil's heart and mind. "I'll have to speak with Pierre again." she began to herself. "And this time, clear things up once and for all." she confirmed, ready to face the challenges coming her way.

***

Casey was feeling like he had been defrauded, that the work and commitment he had put into Val's would be all for nothing. "These assholes should be lucky to have someone like me." he would constantly repeat to himself. "How dare Valeria just up and demote me, and for what? It's not like I've done anything wrong." he sighed. "Last I checked it was I who got the promotion a year ago, is she seriously holding me accountable for that fuckass fire? I know for a damn fact I turned off the fryers and stoves, how could she just blame me? And it's not just her, it's those other assholes too - looking at me like I'm some kind of loser? NEVER in my life have I been treated so terribly." he continued, playing with his feathered earrings. "They'll all come to learn that I am not the one to mess with." he chuckled nefariously.

    By the time everyone had left Val's to go about their day, Casey remained behind at the restaurant. "Let's see how they all manage *without* a fully functioning kitchen." he sneakily said to himself. "It would be a shame if things started to go missing..." he figured. "It would be so tragic if another fire were to 'accidentally' occur". He proceeded, grabbing the whip cream canisters, knives, and bowls - preparing to dispose of them. "Doesn't that she devil know you can buy whipped cream pre made? What a dumb bitch." he critiqued, looking at the metallic canisters that Valeria and the rest of the staff would use to make the dessert topping in house. Tch." he shrugged, now looking at the three mandolin slicers on the shelves. "You little fuckers are next." he pointed, before heading out to the dumpster.

When Valeria announced the year prior that it would be Casey who'd receive the special promotion - the rest of the staff was shocked, but not Casey - he knew this would happen. To Casey, it was a given that a man of his caliber would be rightfully given the position he was destined for. "Not like these other fools could meet me at my level. Heh." he concluded. There was more to Casey's promotion, though he loved to glance over the fact and act as though he had earned it through his own hard work.

Returning to the kitchen, Casey grabbed the two mandolin slicers that were on the shelf and took them out back to dump them. "She did this to herself, actually." he said to himself. He threw the remaining items away and wiped his hands off as though he had just gotten away with murder, once again returning to the kitchen.

"What the-?" he questioned, looking at a stovetop that had been turned on. "Alright, this place has faulty wiring, I knew I wasn't responsible." he shook his head. "Fuckers blamed me, and for what? Faulty wiring!?" He walked over to turn the stove off.

The sound of feet running across the floor caught his attention as he quickly turned around to see what was causing the noise.

"Alright asshole, show yourself, this isn't funny. I'm sure we can talk things over." he shouted, sure that someone had caught him sabotaging the kitchen.

There was no response.

Casey caught the glimpse of a shadowy silhouette reflecting against the lights coming from behind the door leading into the dining room. "Busted, motherfucker." he smirked, speed walking to the door to catch whoever it was. "Gotcha!" he said, quickly looking behind the door - but there was nobody there. "Ha ha, very funny Pierre. Are you trying to get one over on me? Are you that much of a flaming pussy?" he mocked aloud. More footsteps could be heard running again from behind, and as he turned to look - nothing. "This little footwork of yours won't scare me, bitch!" he shouted walking back to the center of the kitchen. "Show yourself you fucking coward. I'm right here, ready to beat your ass into next week." he smirked, with his arms wide open. "Helloooo!?"

In response to his claims, a pair of hands ripped the earrings from Casey's ears, causing a drizzle of blood to begin dripping from his ears down to the floor. "AGH!" he screamed in pain, looking behind him, to find nothing. "You stupid piece of shit, I'll kill you!" he screamed in agony and frustration. When he turned around, a burned and tethered silhouette-like figure faced him, hands behind its back. "And who the fuck are you? Michael fucking Myers? Pussy!" He insulted the figure.

The Silhouette, in response, took a metal skewer from the counter with its one free hand and poked it into Casey's left eye, before putting the hand behind its back.

"What the fuck dude!?" he screamed in pain, trying to take the skewer out. Casey, now knowing he was in danger, tried to run to the door. He could only see from one eye, as tears of blood began rapidly pouring down, a pain that felt like a trip to the optometrist had gone wrong.

The Silhouette aggressively and firmly walked after Casey, revealing a mandolin slicer that they were holding behind their back. They then proceeded to wrap their arms with the slicer around the front of Casey's neck, stopping him in his place, similarly to a prey caught in a predator's trap. "W-what the hell? I-s this really necessary? What'd I do? I'm sorry!" he cried, a mixture of tears and blood running down his face. Casey was beyond petrified, as if at that moment he knew he had messed up and all hope for escape was fleeing from his mind. He was cautious, knowing that one wrong move could end him completely.

The killer proceeded to push the slicer against his neck and repeatedly began slicing his neck back and forth, as Casey began coughing up blood as the mandolin got stuck on pieces of his skin, like a zipper caught on a jacket. The Silhouette continued and forcefully kept slicing, ripping off pieces of Casey's flesh. The more the killer sliced into Casey's throat, the more entangled in the flesh the mandolin became. Nevertheless, the Silhouette continued to slice, akin to a butcher dealing with a difficult piece of fatty meat. Blood began dripping to the floor as the killer finally released the pressure they had on Casey - him falling to the floor, barely clinging to life. Casey felt anger and disgust at this moment, as though his life were flashing before his eyes, and as if he regretted not doing more to punish Valeria and the rest of the staff. Casey's attempts at breathing grew increasingly difficult as he choked on his blood, his neck being ripped apart.

"I don't deserve this." he thought in pain. "I'm supposed to be the next top chef of the culinary world!" he thought to himself, no longer able to speak.

The Silhouette slightly tilted their head, indicating surprise that Casey was still alive. As Casey began to try and crawl away, the killer forcefully turned Casey over, as he began to fully choke on his blood, unable to move anymore. Still not pleased with the results, the Silhouette stomped on Casey's neck repeatedly until he stopped moving completely. After a few moments, the choking stopped and Casey was dead, the darkness that was looming over Val's fully engulfing the kitchen.

Chapter Four

The Ballad of a Burning Man

Darren never predicted that a year after his life had turned around for the worse that he'd return to Amber Creek. Similar to many, the town had hooked its claws on him, leaving him with the painful scars of past traumas. His car was packed to the brim, with Darren hunched over in the tiny vehicle that looked more like a clown car than anything else - however the only fool leaving the vehicle was him.

There was speculation that Valeria Swifton would be returning to the culinary scene- tips left to him by his former mentor's old friends. "This is for you, Redmond." he said to himself, as though he were giving himself a boost in confidence, reassurance that he was making the right move to return to Amber Creek. Even if he hadn't acquired every piece of the puzzle, Darren figured he'd put enough pieces together to figure out the truth: that Valeria Swifton murdered Redmond Thatcher. To Darren, this was the most logical conclusion he could come to, given the heaping insurance policy Valeria had taken out mere days before the fire. "She'll have to answer for her sins." he said to himself with disgust. "But where do I begin? *How* do I begin?" he slouched back in his car, looking to his rearview mirror and staring into his own deep blue eyes. Darren sat in the parking lot of the newly reconstructed Val's, staking out the restaurant in his tinted red sedan. He stayed parked, waiting for any indication that there was something unlawful or suspicious going on for the next two and a half hours.

  After Redmond had died in the fire, it was ruled a kitchen "accident" by the police - a ruling that never sat right with Darren. "There's no way." he shook his head. When he had gone to the police with the evidence he had acquired - the insurance policy, the bills Valeria had fallen behind on, and the scathing review Redmond had left behind - they shrugged him off and dismissed Darren's concerns. To him, it was evident:

Valeria murdered Redmond, as his review would have been the final nail in the coffin for her career.

As time continued to pass, and after dozing off for a few moments, Darren was awoken by a knock at his car's window. Startled, he jumped up and brushed his clothes off before rolling the window down.

"Darren? What're you doing here?" a familiar, green haired woman questioned.

"B-Basil! H-hi! Well, uh, it's funny running into you here of all places!" he panicked, completely unprepared for the interaction. It had been months since he had last spoken to his old high school best friend, though, this could be something Darren could use for his favor.

"...Well, I work here, so it doesn't really seem all that odd to find me here." Basil pointed out.

"Oh...I see..." Daren said, disappointed. "I didn't think *she* would come back." he sighed to himself.

"But again, I ask - what are you doing here, Darren?" she prodded.

"Well..." Darren didn't know how to answer, he was completely taken aback. "You see..."

"I see…? You've been here for the past two hours or so, I saw your car when I arrived."

"Oh, you did? Well…" he was stalling, trying to figure out an excuse for his stakeout, not wanting to alert Basil to his true purpose for being there. "Damn, when it comes to her, she's always been my weak spot." he thought to himself.

"Darren?"

"I'm looking for a job, you see." he made up an excuse.

"…A job? …Really?" Basil said in disbelief.

"Yes! Well, I heard Valeria was reopening her restaurant, and the last year had been exceptionally tough on me, and I thought that just maybe…" his voice trailed off.

"I think I understand now." Basil sighed, nodding her head.

"Well, you should've said something sooner. Why did you just wait out here?

"I may have been a little nervous, you know, considering who my last boss was." he excused.

"Right…" Basil responded. "Well, we just got done for the day, and Valeria is a bit preoccupied with preparations for the soft opening at the moment. Why not come back tomorrow morning? I'll put in a good word for you, I'm sure she'd really appreciate another helping hand." Basil suggested.

"You'd really do that for me?" Darren said with a hint of surprise in his voice, not expecting Basil to go to bat for him.

"Of course I would, we're old friends, aren't we?" she smiled, before looking away for a moment. "And aside from that, it's the least I could do, for not checking in with you more often…" she explained.

"Basil…" Darren affectionately responded. "Thank you, truly." he smiled.

There was a small pause, before either said another word.

"Hey, so I have to get going now, I gotta check in with a friend, but I'd love to catch up with you soon."

"Yeah…No problem, Basil. How about later this week?" Darren asked.

"That sounds good, we'll talk soon!" Basil nodded.

"Talk to you later!" he answered back, with Basil turning to walk back to her car.

Though this encounter was unexpected, Darren realized that perhaps it was divine intervention, as if the universe were trying to guide him towards the path, he needed to take in order to get his answers, to get Redmond justice. "If I get in at Val's..." he began. "...I would have an easier time finding out the truth of that night. Perfect!" he exclaimed to himself. "For Redmond, I'll partake in this song and dance." he affirmed, before driving off to his hotel room.

***

Gianna lived at the Lakenrock Apartment complex, one of Amber Creek's luxury set of apartment homes. Located nearly seven minutes from Val's, Gianna lived at a location central to most of the amenities of Amber Creek. Newly built, the Lakenrock's five buildings stood at five floors tall a piece, with around 15 apartments per floor.

"Apartment 3-57." Basil spoke to herself, reading the directions Gianna had texted her. "How do people not get lost in a place like this?" she pondered, getting all turned around by the complex. Basil had never been the best person to ask for directions, nor was she the one people would turn to when they got lost. "Where is 3-57?" she texted Gianna.

"Building 3, fifth floor." Gianna responded. "Need me to come down?"

"No, I got it." Basil texted back, entering building 3.

The bottles of alcohol rocked against the pints of ice cream in Basil's tote bag. "Can't hide the evidence I suppose." she rolled her eyes, surrendering on her attempts to silence the amount of noise she was making entering the elevator.

The hallways were floored with brown marble that shined brilliantly against the warmth of the wall lights. The walls were soft and golden, with darker strips of gold stripes going down in patterns.

"Good stuff, Gianna. I'm impressed." Basil smirked, exiting the elevator and walking towards the end of the hall, where Gianna's door was open and she stood out, waiting for Basil to arrive.

"Hey stranger, come here often?" Gianna teased, welcoming Basil in.

"Didn't expect to find a cutie like you in a place like this." Basil joked back, giving Gianna a hug.

Basil put the drinks and ice cream away and took a seat on Gianna's black leather couch. Her apartment was decorated elegantly, with new furniture and tv sets throughout the entire space. There were framed pictures on the wall, mostly from the past and a few that Basil could recognize. "Hey, is that...?" she pointed to one of the framed pictures, getting up from the couch and walking to it.

"Feels like yesterday, doesn't it, Basil?" Gianna responded to the picture, as she poured the two a glass of wine.

"My god, we look so young here!" Basil gasped.

"Yeah, Harold even had a few strands of hair left!" Gianna teased, to which Basil chuckled.

"What was this? Five years ago?"

"Right on the marker as always, B."

"I can't believe just how fast time flies by, it's crazy to think about. Makes you really value the time you have now." Basil commented. "So how are you?" she asked, turning back to sit next to Gianna who was now on the couch.

"Could be better, but fine I guess." Gianna shrugged. "I should be asking you that, especially after..." her voice trailed

"It's fine, we can talk about it." Gianna assured her.

    There was a large part of Basil that was curious as to what exactly happened in the year she was gone. With a mixture of anger and concern, she was desperately wanting to find out why Pierre started acting the way he did earlier. It was

a shame, Basil felt, that the close-knit bond she had with Gianna and Pierre was slowly beginning to untangle into a mess of string. "I have to fix this." she thought to herself.
"Then, if you don't mind me asking, what exactly happened?"
"I don't know entirely myself, if I'm being perfectly honest. Something went down between him and Casey the night Val's burned down, that much I know. For the first few weeks, he seemed to be doing pretty alright, but once you left, something shifted. He's never been fond of change, so maybe with so much happening at once, it was too much for him."
"So he resorted to alcoholism?" Basil questioned.
"Hey, we all have our own ways to cope with the shit that bothers us." Gianna defended.
"But didn't that have a direct effect on the two of you as well?"
"Yeah…I guess…But still, I made the decision to help him, it's not like anyone else was around to help out."

There was a short silence.
"…Nobody helped?" Basil awkwardly asked.
"None. Not a single soul. Couldn't tell you why, really. Valeria disappeared, Emorie left to go find herself with Alejandro, and Harold retired and moved off to Red Moon Falls. And Casey,

well, let's just say Pierre wanted nothing to do with that motherfucker."

"Damn, tell me how you really feel."

"That piece of shit continued to torment Pierre; it drove him fuckin nuts." Gianna began. "Don't get me wrong, I thought about the many ways I could torment Pierre too, given all he's done. But at the end of the day, he's still one of my closest friends, regardless of our complicated history."

"No, no, I understand you completely. I only wish that I did more myself…"

"Bah! Don't beat yourself up over it, at least you genuinely care. That's more than I can say for the others…"

"What about his limp? I noticed he started walking differently."

"Oh! And that's another thing!"

"What do you mean by that?"

"That fucking hippie! About three months ago, Casey was up to his usual bullshit and giving Pierre a hard ass time, and mind you, the man was as drunk as you can imagine. Feather brain knew this, so he purposefully went poking around and riled him up.

"Then what happened?"

"They got into this huge fight. Fists went swinging, chairs were thrown, and glass mugs were shattered. Casey got the upper hand on Pierre and stomped down on his ankle."

"Oh my god!? What the fuck!?"

"Yeah! That's what I fucking said too! When the cops showed up, they took the bastard's side because the bartender said that Pierre made the first swing! Ridiculous! It's not Pierre's fault that the hippie antagonized him! And for what!? What the hell did Pierre do!? Now he has a busted ankle."

"I can't believe Casey would do something like that!" Basil said enraged, though she knew it wasn't entirely Casey's fault. There was more to the story, like what happened the night Val's burned down to cause the friendship between the two men to sour. And more importantly, if Pierre hadn't become such a raging drunk, would that altercation have occurred in the first place? Regardless, Basil was more of a friend to Gianna and Pierre than she was to Casey, and Basil would side with her two closest friends versus that of the slacker who is full of himself.

"I'm surprised Valeria let the asshole back, I'll tell you that. I'd kill him ten times over before I let Casey back in the kitchen. He started the fire; you know that right? It's his fault the Red guy's dead."

"You really think so?"

"No doubt about it, Basil. Casey's as careless as rats get, and he was the last one to leave the kitchen before we closed it up.

Basil was doubtful over the allegations Gianna made over Casey, as she looked back to the night Val's burned down, and to the silhouette-like figure she saw fleeing the scene.

"Gianna?"

"Yeah?"

"I don't think Casey burned the restaurant down, if I'm being honest." Basil confided.

"Are you sure about that? It seems pretty obvious to me."

"I saw something that night. Something I haven't talked to anyone about."

"What do you mean you saw something? Like an explosion?" Gianna shot up from her seat, the wine in her glass shaking around.

"There was a man."

"A man?"

"Or woman, I don't really know if I'm being honest."

"Yeah, it was probably Casey leaving the scene of the crime." Gianna persisted.

"No, they were wearing something over their face, I couldn't quite make out the entire figure. Only a silhouette."

"A silhouette? Are you sure you weren't just hallucinating? Trying to make something out of nothing?" Gianna doubted.

But there was no doubt in Basil's mind that there was more to what happened that night than any of them could know. She's fearful, however, fearful over the possibility that there was an arsonist lurking around - a potential murderer. This concept frightened Basil, who chose to remain silent for all this time out of concern that the silhouette she saw would find her and silence her. It's for this reason that Gianna is the only person Basil's spoken to about this. Gianna, however, seemed to not believe what Basil was trying to explain, and was more satisfied with the idea that Casey was the true culprit. "Whatever happened that night, it's taken a toll on all of us, on some harder than most." she thought to herself, concerned over the fates of her coworkers and friends. "I have to do something about this." she concluded. "For Gianna, and for Pierre. I'll unmask the truth, and dance my way through the kitchen like Valeria, and rescue them from this rut they've gotten themselves into." she affirmed to herself.

"Hey, you want another glass?" Gianna asked.

"Sure, I'll take another." Basil responded, with Gianna refilling both of their cups and changing the conversation.

***

It alarmed Darren just how quickly Valeria had rebuilt her restaurant. Standing near the front of Val's, Darren looked up at the newly remodeled building, disgusted by the graveyard of a restaurant. Arriving at nearly nine forty-five in the morning, the cars of the other employees had arrived much sooner - Basil included. There were walls of doubt surrounding Darren's mind, fears and concerns that Valeria would not allow the former protege of Redmond Thatcher to work under her - given what he knows. "It's your play, Valeria." he thought to himself.

Despite the emptiness of the restaurant, a symphony of noise gave the illusion that the building was crowded. The sounds of employees in the kitchen shouting at each other and bantering echoed throughout the dining hall. The light from the sun and sky shined through the clear, glass roof and filled the environment with a feeling of warmth and comfort. "This place is something else." Darren scoffed.

"...Oh? A guest?" a blonde woman's voice questioned. "Sorry, but we're not open right now, and we won't be for a while longer." she explained.

"Oh! Well.." Darren stuttered.

"Don't tell me, you're with those fuck heads across the street, aren't you?" she questioned with growing impatience.

"What's going on here!?" Darren muttered fearfully. "No, you have it all wrong, you see-"

"Ms. McKnight! What're you doing? Who are you talking to?" an older male voice questioned, walking up to the woman.

"We have work to do, get back into the kitchen!"

"What? Harold! I was just--"

"I don't want to hear it, young lady! Remember what's at stake!" He scolded, signaling for her to return to the kitchen. The man, who Darren heard was named Harold, turned to Darren and looked him up and down."

"Ah yes, I remember you well young man." he nodded.

"Y-you do?" Darren asked, tensing up.

"Well yes, you are an associate of Mr. Thatcher, are you not? You visited our establishment well over a year ago."

"W-wow, I didn't think you'd remember me. My name is Darren Pierce, it's a pleasure to meet you..." Darren walked over to Harold to shake his hand.

"...Dunbar, Harold Dunbar. But you may just call me Harold." he introduced, returning the handshake with a firm grip. "Strong shake. I can tell you are a strong man, Mr. Pierce." he observed.

"T-thanks."

"Now all we need to do is work on that jumpiness of yours." Harold laughed off. "You can calm down boy, we aren't savages!"

"I'll try." Darren awkwardly said, attempting to just go along with the conversation.

"I was told you came in for an interview with Valeria, you also came highly recommended by one of our finest staff members."

"Basil..." Darren spoke softly to himself. "...she remembered!" he gleefully expressed, before returning back to the conversation with Harold. "I did! I was hoping for an opportunity to introduce myself and have a conversation with her, if that's alright."

"Follow me to the back of the kitchen, we can go ahead and introduce you to the Chef and get you set up right away."

"Set me up?"

"To be frank, and you didn't hear this from me, but one of our veteran staff members didn't show up to work today - a real hassle. Stole several equipment items and just left without so much as a two-week notice!"

"Really?" Darren questioned in a surprised tone. "That sounds terrible, and to pass on such a great opportunity such as this!" he finished, entering the kitchen.

"My thoughts exactly!" Harold agreed. "With that in mind, I have a feeling that Valeria will be keen to have you on board." he kindly assured a still nervous Darren.

Darren looked to the grand kitchen, which looked like a completely different atmosphere from that of its former self. The kitchen itself was bright, with stovetops, cutting stations, ovens, and fryers encapsulating the area. Regardless of how he felt about the woman, Darren recognized just how extravagant and well put together Valeria's kitchen was, a testament to the quality of her craft.

"Yo! Darren!" a familiar voice echoed, it was Alejandro, another face Darren hadn't seen in a year.

"Hey! Long time no see!" Darren returned the greeting.

Darren tried to say hello to Basil, however she was consumed by her work - preparing produce to be used during the soft opening. Mrs. McKnight, who Darren didn't get off on the right foot with, only gave Darren daggers, forming meat patties and other items, as though she were saying something along the lines of "If you fool around or do something stupid, I'll kill you and squish you like these patties." This thought terrified Darren, and thereby made him fearful of her.

"Excuse me, Ms. Wallace, do you have a moment?" Harold questioned a younger woman with a black pixie cut.

"Yes? What is it, Harold?" she turned and asked.

"Mr. Pierce here has arrived for an interview with Valeria - is she available?"

"Not at the moment, no, she's out for the time being. However, she entrusted me with the responsibility to see if Basil's friend is up to the challenge. You can leave him with me." she instructed, ushering for Harold to leave, and giving a short smile to Darren. "It's a pleasure, my name is Emorie Wallace, I am Valeria's second in command. Pleased to meet you, I've heard many great things." she greeted, giving Darren a soft handshake.

"Darren Pierce, it's a pleasure." he said, as they both returned to the dining hall to conduct the interview.

***

Basil was troubled by the fact that she didn't have an opportunity to greet Darren, though she figured that she'd see him again soon enough. "There's something I need to bring up to him about that night." she had concluded. "But first…" she looked over at Pierre, who was facing away from her. "I need to fix this." she realized.

Before she could walk over to Pierre, in hopes he wouldn't blow up on her in front of the entire staff, Basil was cut off by Emorie, who returned to the kitchen with a pleasant expression.

"Emorie, hi!" Basil jumped.

"Basil, I just finished the interview with Darren, I thought you'd like to know!"

"Oh! How'd it go? How'd he do?"

"I thought you'd be pleased to know he was an excellent candidate! And given what happened with Casey being a no call no show, the job is looking to be his. I just need to confirm a few things with Valeria, and he should be ready to go."

"That's great!" Basil gleefully responded. "He'll fit right in with us, I'm sure of it!"

"I'd have to agree with you there." Emorie responded. "I have to get back to work now, but thank you again for your dedication to Val's, it is noticed and appreciated!" she nodded, before turning back to resume her work.

  A sense of relief washed over Basil, with Darren's hiring and Emorie's words of reassurance giving her a stronger attachment to the hope that she might actually get the promotion she had missed out on. "They believe in me." she affirmed to herself. "Now if I could only believe in myself." she concluded, continuing her way to Pierre.

"Pierre!" Basil called out, to which Pierre ignored her. "Hey, I know you can hear me, I'm talking to you!" she said closer to Pierre, respecting their privacy and hoping to keep the conversation solely between the two of them.

"Hmph." was the only sound Pierre would make.

"Well, fine. You don't have to talk, just listen, if only for a second. I know that we have some problems we need to work out, and I think it's safe to say that we both handled a lot of things very poorly. I want to talk it out. Tomorrow evening, at the Hartsgrove Apartment spaces, I'll meet you at the pool at eight o'clock." She handed him a key card. "You can use this to get in. Don't feel pressured to show up or anything, but I hope you do, Pierre." she finished, before walking back to her station.

    Basil had no idea whether or not Pierre would show up tomorrow night, however she extended the olive branch in hopes that they could mend the broken bridges of their friendship. She was concerned for Pierre - worried over the attitude he had taken on, and also for the direction his life was going. Though that may be the case, Basil also recognized that there wouldn't be much she could do if Pierre refused to let her in, and so she understood that she had to handle this situation with much delicacy. "I can do this." she said to herself, as she continued to use the mandolin slicer to dice up some onions.

Chapter Five

From the Void, Comes Repentance

The three days Basil had been back in Amber Creek had felt more like an eternity, making Basil wonder if time was standing still. Basil almost felt that it wouldn't be such a bad thing if that were the case, with her being worried that there wouldn't be enough time for her to mend her broken relationship with Pierre before the soft opening of Val's. "I can't think like this." she said to herself, slapping herself back to reality. "Tonight, will go exactly as it needs to, and I'll do everything I can to ensure this." she proclaimed, falling back down on her bed.

Basil's apartment felt more like a loft, given how small the space she rented out was. There weren't many move-in ready options available for her when she got Valeria's call,

Hartsgrove was the only option. The biggest perk, Basil felt, was the lack of noisy neighbors - with the walls being nearly soundproof. Amber Creek was a town known for its luxury which came in every different shape and size and ensured that wherever Basil ended up, she would be fine. Her apartment was filled to the brim with furniture: an oversized couch that almost overtook the entire space, a dining room table clearly meant for a much larger dining room, and a bed fit for at least three - all of which made the space feel a tad bit cramped. Basil had figured that once things had smoothed over, that she would be able to have everyone over, that her apartment could become a safe space for her friends and coworkers. To Basil, this was extremely important, to be the type of person people could depend on and feel protected with. Taking a heavy sigh, Basil rose up from her bed and looked around at her vacuous home. "Something's not right." she felt. Sadness overtook her emotions, making her feel hollow and incomplete. "Gianna's place felt so warm, why doesn't mine?" she sighed. "What am I doing wrong?" she questioned.

    Deciding not to dwell on these thoughts any longer, Basil stood up and stretched, before nodding. "Right. I need to get started - seek out answers as to what happened last year." she said aloud to herself. A large part of Basil hoped that Gianna's doubt was correct, that there wasn't something else at play and that the fire was just an accident and nothing more. Basil didn't want to believe that someone would resort to such extreme levels of violence, and for what? It didn't make any sense to her. "Perhaps Casey's absence yesterday was evidence enough, maybe he left out of guilt." she tried to justify. "Regardless, I need to know for certain. This back-and-forth speculation won't do me an ounce of good, the facts will tell me all I need to know." she concluded, grabbing her keys and heading out her door.

***

Since their argument in the alley, Gianna and Pierre had not spoken a word to each other. This partly bothered Gianna, who had thought Pierre would come to her with an apology. "It's the least he could do." she huffed. Her feelings were hurt, and Gianna could feel it in her heart that things would never return to how they used to be with Pierre, causing her stomach to feel twisted and turned in knots. When Basil first showed up, she truthfully had no idea how she would feel - whether it be angry at her for leaving, envy, jealousy, or even resentment. However, these worries subsided the moment she saw Basil again, as if all of the good they had experienced together flooded her memories like a hurricane out of season. "How could I be mad at her for moving on? She did better than I ever could." she felt. "But Pierre..." Gianna was having a difficult time trying to stay mad at Pierre, as though he had an iron tight grip on her soul that refused to let her stay angry with him. "...He's been acting super weird, weirder than normal." she sighed with concern. "Something's up." she strongly felt.

Initially, Gianna paid no attention to the concerns brought up by Basil the night before, dismissing her kooky claims of a masked figure being responsible for the fire. "I love her to death, but that girl has a wild imagination." she expressed. "Although..." she began, momentarily entertaining the idea. "A ghostly silhouette sounds too ridiculous to be real." she concluded.

There was, however, a disturbing feeling that she was being watched, more precisely, being followed. This suspicion followed Gianna as she walked through the aisles of the supermarket, turning in and out of each aisle to see if there really was a stalker following her. "Could this be?" she thought. "Must be imagining things." she said to herself, as she continued to the produce section. Gianna looked all around her, seeking to identify any recognizable faces. She didn't want to make a scene in public either, so Gianna couldn't just scream and curse out into the void like she wanted to do. With this feeling growing more and more scary by the minute, Gianna couldn't focus on shopping and instead chose to abandon her cart and quickly leave the store. "I'm gonna get in my car, go home, and that'll be the end of it." she said to herself, speedily walking through the busy parking lot to try to find her car. "Fuck! Where did I park!?" she panicked, searching for her keys in her purse, and not watching where she was going.

 As Gianna blindly walked through the parking lot, her misplaced focus was interrupted by an arm reaching out to grab her. Before she had the chance to scream, the aggressive sound of a car honking brought her back to the present, with another woman in a large SUV cursing Gianna out and flipping her off.

"Go fuck yourself!" Gianna screamed back, despite being in the wrong. "Your kids are ugly!" she screamed, signaling to the woman's two children in the backseat. Before any more words were spoken, the woman drove away, shrugging Gianna's words off. "Now who-?" Gianna began to ask, in regard to the arms that pulled her away from the traffic.

"No no, this won't do at all." a familiar, grating voice chastised from behind Gianna. "Honestly, this hothead of yours is going to get you in trouble one day."

"And who says I don't like trouble?" Gianna scoffed, turning around to find Heather Madden. "It's you!" she began.

"Well of course, who else would it be?"

"You're the creepy bitch that's been following me!"

"Whatever do you mean, dear Gianna?" Heather asked, with a sliver of concern in her voice. "Has someone been stalking you?"

"Don't play dumb, Heather. If it wasn't you, then where the hell is Marcellus? Behind every evil, is an even more twisted, insidious, and dark persona. Where is the man?"

"Your words never fail to make me laugh." Heather chuckled. "I haven't seen him at all today, unfortunately for you. I'm afraid he would've jumped on you the moment he heard what you just said. Now shall we step out of traffic for a moment to talk?"

"And why should I?"

"Because I've been followed too, since I returned to Amber Creek."

Gianna found her car and unlocked it, signaling for Heather to get in. Though she had doubts over Heather's claims, she figured it wouldn't do her any harm in hearing her out, especially if it was true that there was a stalker.

"I want to preface this by saying that running into you happened by mere coincidence, I had other reasons for being in the area and just so happened to see you almost get hit by that car." Heather began.

"Sure, I believe ya…NOT!" Gianna responded.

"At least hear me out." Heather expressed. "I understand we have our grievances; however I fear that what's going on right now should be the most important topic at hand." she continued.

"Since when does Heather talk like this?" Gianna questioned, reflecting on all of their previous interactions.

"It all started when I returned to town a couple of days ago, I received a letter directly addressed to me at my hotel room. Initially, I had assumed it was Marcellus, however when I opened the letter…" Heather took the envelope out from her purse and handed it to Gianna. "Take a look at it for yourself."

Gianna opened the letter to read its contents, and all that was written was a message in red reading "LEAVE NOW". This alarmed Gianna, who jumped back at the ominous message, though doubt immediately entered her mind.

"And how can I believe you didn't write this yourself? This could all just be a ploy to get in good with the staff of Val's."

"A very understandable claim, however there's more to this, trust me." Heather pleaded. "Now, I wanted your thoughts on the possibility of there being a third party involved with the fire that killed Redmond Thatcher last year."

"A third party? Are you fucking serious?" Gianna's eyebrow raised.

"You see, a part of my reasoning for returning had nothing to do with writing a hit piece on Val's, I returned based on a second letter I received from an individual who wishes to remain anonymous, explaining to me that there may have been someone else behind last year's incident."

"Yeah, it was Casey. Are you slow?"

"And have you seen Casey in the last few days?"

"I saw him the day of our meeting, after that the rat got up and left town. He stole a bunch of equipment too, the ungrateful bastard."

"He left town, you say?"

"Yeah, he was a no call no show yesterday. It was unbelievable, Emorie and Valeria were PISSED."

"What if I told you his car and belongings were all still at his home? There's evidence to prove that he hasn't left town at all."

"Probably hitched a ride with some girl, the man is a total fucking player. Keep up please." Gianna said with irritation in her voice. "First Basil, and now you? What's up with everyone lately?" she questioned.

"Basil? Did something happen to her?"

"She brought up the same idea you just did, that someone else was responsible for the fire."

"She did? How was she so certain!?"

"She claimed to have seen a silhouette," Gianna paused. "Wait a minute, why the hell am I telling you all this? All you're gonna do is turn around and use this shit against me, aren't you? God I'm such a sucker, Valeria would murder me if she saw that I was talking to you"

"Gianna, that's not what I'm trying to do, I can assure you-"

"And you can assure that I'll beat your ass if you come and bother me again. Look, I was probably just overthinking earlier and let my stress get to me. Everything will be fine."

"But Gianna-"

"Get out of my car, tweedle dumb!" Gianna barked, to which Heather reluctantly obeyed.

"My card." Heather handed it to Gianna, who took it, and tore it up in front of Heather.

"Here's what I think about your card!" she mocked.

"Very well, Gianna. Do take care of yourself." Heather solemnly responded, before turning and walking away.

"Fuck this." Gianna said with a sigh and a deep breath. "Was Basil, right?" she began thinking to herself. "Differences aside, Heather mentioned a few things that'd line up with what Basil was saying. But what was up with her? She seemed so completely out of character. What exactly has she been up to?" she questioned with suspicion. "Never mind that, I still gotta..." her voice trailed off. "...go to a *different* store." she finished, leaving her questions and worries in the parking lot.

***

Some parts of Alejandro felt guilty about the situation he found himself in. Not by chance, but by choice, he stood at a crossroads - needing to make a quick second decision about his next move. The alley smelled of garbage and rotten eggs, and the pungent aura was amplified by the man standing before him.

"So, what is it gonna be?" a flamboyant, male voice questioned.

"I'm thinking about it, gimme a sec." Alejandro responded.

"Times up, I need an answer, sweetheart. You called me out here on my day off all hush hush, I expected you to be a little...*more*."

"More?"

"Yeah, you know...More..." the man made a gesture with his hands in a spinning motion. "...More exciting, I guess."

"I can see why Gianna doesn't like you, Marcellus. You leave a lot to be desired."

"Oh, I can show you *desire*." Marcellus assured Alejandro.

Despite working under Valeria, and being the newest hire of the veteran staff, Alejandro felt minimal allegiance to those he worked with. It bothered him greatly that the chef he had looked up to for so long was not the icon she was painted out to be. "Someone like her, promoting *him*? I call bull." he complained, reflecting on the prior year's promotion. "Any one of us would have been a better pick. It's an insult - to me, the staff, and especially Emorie." he continued to himself. For Alejandro, who had spent the entirety of the last year with Emorie, he had an immense respect for the sous chef. The longer he spent with her the more he began to realize just how insulting it was for Casey to even be in the same kitchen as her. "And after what I saw…" he continued. "…it's disgusting to think about."

"Okay, I'm willing to work with you, so long as my help remains anonymous. I'll kill ya if you tell another soul." Alejandro threatened.

"Wow, what a strong, brave man. I'm soaking wet from the intimidation!" Marcellus mockingly gasped. "Still though, I am quite surprised that you would sell Valeria down the river so fast. To me, nonetheless." Marcellus admitted. "And don't you worry a pretty little hair about a pretty little thing, okay? I kept our little rendezvous here a secret, from Heather too, so I can assure you that this will be our pretty little secret." he winked.

"Ugh." Alejandro shivered in disgust. "And about what you just said, let's just say that if anybody sees this," he began, holding up a manila envelope filled with heavy paper. "Valeria will be finished," he continued, handing Marcellus the envelope.

"Oh em gee!?" Marcellus squealed. "And these are real photos? Are you sure?"

"Took 'em myself, but I never thought I'd have the opportunity to use these."

"Well, I can guarantee I will paint the town red with these. Hoo hoo, perfect! Ha ha!" Marcellus celebrated. "I must thank you again for your service, Alejandro. And once this scandal blows over, I will personally extend an invitation for you, and that lady friend of yours to work at my restaurant. We can make history, the three of us. We'll destroy Valeria."

"Ehh, I'll think about it, just make sure the world sees the exact kind of monster Valeria Swifton is." Alejandro shrugged. "Can I ask about something before I go?"

"Anything for you, pretty boy. Shoot."

"I have my reasons for doing what I'm doing, but what about you?"

"Me? Well, I guess you could say it's a wee bit complicated. But to make a long story short, let's just say *that* she devil betrayed me and left me for dead." he nefariously smiled. "But in the end, all shall be right." Marcellus chuckled. "She'll regret her sins." he finished.

"...Okay then..." Alejandro awkwardly laughed along, unsure of how to respond. To him, Marcellus sounded cringey and too high and mighty. Regardless, he knew that Valeria's rival would be able to assist him in taking down Valeria. "I'll talk to you soon." Alejandro said, shaking Marcellus' hand with a firm grip and leaving the alleyway.

Alejandro got in his car, and drove off, turning four blocks over before parking in the lot of Val's, pondering his next move as he stared at the restaurant sign.

***

Basil looked at her phone, which read "7:00 P.M" and figured she had enough time to check for clues at one location, given how close she lived to Val's. "I can keep looking tomorrow, but for now..." she gulped. "I'll test my luck here." She looked up at the building which read "AMORE" and then to the empty parking lot. "Nobody's here right now, which means it's the perfect time to check this place out. But how will I get in?" she wondered, looking for a way in. "The front and back entrances are locked, so..." She turned to look at the side of the building, hoping to find something. "Oh! Perfect!" she exclaimed, eyes facing the vent leading into the restaurant. "I can fit in." she said with confidence. Despite her stature, Basil was as resourceful as she was smart and had learned during childhood how to make an entrance if there wasn't one there for her. Though it hadn't been the most ideal, Basil now found herself grateful that the troubled experiences of her past would be able to come in handy at the moment she needed them the most.

Prying the vent open, Basil wiggled her way inside, similar to a worm burrowing underground. The vent was surprisingly spacious, filled with a small village of dust and spiderwebs. "Marcellus, what exactly have you been doing the past year?" she questioned. "If these vents aren't even cleaned, then I wonder what the restaurant itself will look like." As she continued crawling through, she looked down at the open space of the vents to see below her, and saw glimpses of a dark, purple walled eating room with stained carpets. The chairs and tables were covered in a clear plastic wrap, as though the restaurant hadn't been in operation in at least a year. "What's going on here?" she wondered. Basil had suspected that Marcellus could easily be the suspicious silhouette she had seen the night of the fire. Though the origin of their rivalry remained unknown to most, Valeria and Marcellus were known to go at it back and forth. With Val's being right across from Amore, Marcellus saw most of his business disappear to Valeria, which only fueled the resentment that was cooking from within him. "There has to be something here." she said to herself, continuing her way through the vents. The restaurant was dead quiet, which felt somewhat ominous, with Basil unsure if the noises she heard below her were from rodents or something else. Basil saw her opportunity to jump from the vents through the vents above the grill. "This place sure does have some interesting architectural choices." she commented, in regard to how the ventilation system ran through the restaurant. The vent spaces grew narrower as she made her way above the grills, which were normally removable so that kitchen staff could clean and rotate them. The biggest challenge remained though - with the vents being somewhat rusty with grease stains and other unidentifiable marks. "This is so disgusting." she shivered, plugging her nose from the rancid smell. Stretching out her arms in front of her, she attempted to adjust the grill vents for a few moments, successfully dropping one down, making a loud bang noise that reverberated throughout the entire restaurant space. "It's a good thing nobody's here." she awkwardly laughed, as she did the same tactic for the next three vents. Nudging herself forward, Basil leapt out of the vent and banged herself on the grill. "Shit." she complained. "Hurt more than expected." she brushed herself off, sighing at the sight of the stains and marks transferred to her shirt from the vent.

The kitchen was dark, with vents over the ceilings, which Basil assumed was a questionable aesthetic choice. The equipment was not well maintained, with there being stains, spots, and scrapes on the grill, fridges, and cooking stations. If Basil hadn't known better, she'd assume that Amore had been abandoned by Marcellus. Taking out her phone, Basil took photos of the kitchen to record the state she found it in. "How peculiar." she figured, now turning on her phone flashlight, with her phone now reading "7:45 P.M". "I have to hurry for Pierre." she said to herself, setting her sights on the kitchen. She sent a text message to Pierre saying she may be a few minutes late, but unbeknownst to her - she had no service. "Very well, let's begin, shall we?" she took a deep breath, beginning her investigation of Amore.

***

Initially Pierre wasn't going to accept Basil's invitation, but as he began to sober up through the day, he realized the least he could do was hear her out. "It's Basil after all." he dryly smiled, getting out of his car.

The Hartsgrove apartments were nothing special to Pierre, who scoffed at how small the spaces looked. "Seriously? Chef Basil couldn't afford any better?" he complained. "She deserves so much more than this." he sighed, looking for the pool. "I wonder if she had gotten the promotion, would things have turned out differently? Could she and I have…?" his thoughts trailed off. "I need to tell her," He affirmed. "She needs to know that I love her."

Pierre made his way to the pool gate, and scanned the card Basil gave him, taking a seat at the edge of one of the long pool chairs. The area was eerily quiet, with the slightest noise grabbing Pierre's attention. There was pink tarp wrapped around the fences which created a type of wall that left those on the inside of the pool area unable to see out of it, and vice versa. The scuffling of footsteps coming from the outer gates frightened him, as he turned to see where it was coming from. "Basil? That you?" he questioned. There was no response. Pierre looked down at his phone which read "8:05 P.M" "Where is she?" he wondered. The noises he heard earlier grew louder, as he jumped and stood up to look around him. "Alright, not funny!!!" he yelled. "Come on now! Basil!" he continued, looking at a strange shadow reflected on the back of the tarp. "Basil!?"

***

Basil, noticing the time on her phone, knew she had to wrap things up. Given how short of a time frame she had to investigate, she figured that either this was all for nothing, or Marcellus had just kept things well hidden. "Now the question remains..." she started. "...how do I get out?" she pondered, not wanting to go through the vents again, especially with how many webs she still had in her hair. There were roaches and other insects that scurried across the floor, which freaked Basil out. "Spiders, I can handle, but roaches..." she shivered. "Yup, gotta find another way out." she nervously concluded.

The sounds of what Basil believed to be bugs and rodents rang behind her, knocking against the pots and pans, which scared Basil a bit. "Just some rats." she sighed. "Just some rats, just some ra-" The sounds grew louder, which alerted Basil to turn around, but there was nothing but bugs and equipment on the floor. "You're getting worked up over nothing." she gulped. "Maybe there's a set of keys in Marcellus' office." she assumed, walking to his office in the back of the kitchen.

***

As Pierre walked towards the pink tarp to get a good look at what was making so much noise, he jumped back and landed on his butt as a squealing rat poked through the tarp and ran right past him. "Jesus!" he squealed. "Seriously?" he complained, rubbing his ankle.

The clock read "8:20 P.M" and Basil still hadn't shown up, which got Pierre growing increasingly impatient.

***

With a stroke of luck, Basil found a set of spare keys, which would allow Basil to gracefully make her escape, without leaving any signs of a break in. "Oh, thank god." she sighed with relief, making her way back through the kitchen.

Walking through the kitchen, Basil slipped on a puddle of oil that was oozing over the floor. "Shit!" she screeched in moderate pain. "When did this happen?" she questioned. "Did something spill?" she was asked.

All at once, Basil felt a sharp jab coming from her back that sent a shock to her spine, as she began screaming in severe pain. "AH!!" The pain subsided for a moment, as though the pressure on her back was relieved. Putting her hand on her back to try and figure out what it was, all she could feel was a warm, wet substance. Bringing her hands back around, she saw her blood covered hands. Letting out a hug scream, she turned to see her worst nightmare.

The figure that stood before her dropped the knife it was holding, and also reminded Basil of what she had seen the year prior. Its presence was not necessarily scary; however its presence left her with a feeling of great disturbance and trouble. Its chained black trench coat and bloodied, burnt mask reminded Basil of a demon from a horror movie, something sinister and devilish. "I-t's you!" she gasped, as the Silhouette tilted its head. "You were the one who started the fire!" she screamed in growing fear and discomfort, growing weaker by the moment. "I gotta get the hell outta here!" she panicked, turning her back to run towards the front door.

"Help! Anyone! Please!" she screamed into the void. The Silhouette aggressively stomped after her, as Basil pushed pans, chairs, and any other item she could down to block its path. Basil went to one side of a table, with the Silhouette on the other, when she signaled to move left, the Silhouette did the same back and forth. Hoping for a sliver of a chance to escape, Basil broke the loop and tried to make her way to the front door, and panicked to find the right key, as her bloodied hands made it difficult to identify which key was the correct one. "Help me!" she banged on the door, looking over at the empty Val's parking lot across the street. The Silhouette shadowed over her, grabbing her hair and violently pulling her back into the kitchen, her feet no longer able to walk as it just dragged her, banging her against the objects she used to try and originally block its path.

 Back in the kitchen, the Silhouette dropped Basil on the floor and turned her over so she could look up at its tethered and bloodied face. "W-what do you want from me!?" she cried out. "Please! I'm begging you to let me go!" she screamed. "I-I can't die here, they need me!" she pleaded, to a mute Silhouette. "It can't end here." she nervously thought to herself. To her surprise, the Silhouette appeared to have listened to her and walked away, leaving her badly injured on the floor of the kitchen. "T-thank you!" she cried in relief

***

"What the hell? Where is she? It's 8:35, what the fuck!?" Pierre complained. "I knew I shouldn't have given that bitch a chance." Pierre angrily said. "See if I ever give someone the benefit of the doubt again." he complained, saddened by his loneliness.

***

As Basil lay on the floor in agonizing pain and silence, she began to figure out her next move, with her unable to get up from the floor. "I...need to call...the police..." she weakly spoke. Basil's thoughts were interrupted by the Silhouette, who returned with a black duffel bag.
"W-what!? N-no no! Please please please, I beg you!" Basil pleaded.
    The Silhouette rummaged through its bag and took out a large, motorized blade with sharp chains going around it.

To Basil, the item looked like some form of modified meat saw intended to be used as a weapon. She was petrified, feeling worthless and as though there was no hope for her. "This wasn't supposed to happen!" she cried.

Turning the saw on, it made a sound similar to a chainsaw - with the Silhouette swinging it around before standing above Basil.

"Please!!!!!! Don't do thi-" Basil was interrupted by coughs of blood and the sudden emergence of tears as the Silhouette slashed through Basil's stomach, blood and guts spilling out of her stomach. "G-gianna...H-harold...P-pierre. I'm so sorry, I failed y-" before she could finish, the blade made its way up her stomach and through her face as all at once it went quiet and Basil had no more thoughts, laying split open, and dead on the floor.

The Silhouette opened up a cabinet to find an old bag of sugar with bugs inside of it, and sprinkled the sugar over Basil's remains, as the legion of rats and roaches began scuttling towards her corpse, ready for a meal.

***

"Basil…" Pierre was disheartened by Basil being a no show, and a part of him feared that she would never have shown up to begin with. "I guess none of this mattered anyways. That bitch." he said, upset over being what he thought was being stood up. "I need a drink." he whined, angrily leaving the apartments and heading towards a bar.

Chapter Six

The Bonds That Make Us

With two more days until opening, the staff of Val's had been whipped up into a frenzy. With Casey having been a no call no show - expectedly at that - the crew did not feel as if they had taken any real loss, especially considering the hiring of Darren, who surprised everyone with his technical prowess. The largest surprise however for the entire staff would have to be the sudden disappearance of Basil. The morning started out as normal, with the remaining staff members making their way to work - Valeria, Emorie, then Harold and Gianna, followed by Alejandro and Darren, and then finally, Pierre.
"Basil has yet to arrive, hasn't she?" Harold questioned, looking at the watch on his right wrist, which read "9:15 A.M".

"Aren't we gonna learn these new recipes? I thought for sure she'd be here around 8 or so to get ahead of things." Gianna added.

"Just like her to do somethin like this. Tch." Pierre scoffed.

"What's with you?" Gianna asked.

"Ahem." Emorie coughed, breaking up Pierre and Gianna. "This is honestly quite alarming. Casey's one thing, but if we lose Basil too... I cannot accept this." she shook her head in frustration.

Darren was lost in his thoughts, trying to put together the reason Basil had decided not to show up. "No texts, no calls. This is so unlike her." he thought, reminiscing on their time in high school. "Heh. She would wince every time she was late to something, and when the weight of the world fell on her shoulders, Basil would match its strength. C'mon. C'mon." he continued, messaging Basil again and asking where she was.

"Have any of you been able to get in touch with her?" Darren asked the staff.

"I've been calling her for the last half hour, and nothing..." Emorie responded.

"Nothin' to my stuff either." Gianna chimed in.

"Same here." Alejandro added.

"This is very unlike her." Harold confirmed, shaking his head.

"Hmph." An annoyed Pierre huffed, which caught the attention of Gianna.

"What'd you say to her, huh? What'd you do?" Gianna interrogated. "Weren't you supposed to meet up with her last night?" she pushed. "What happened, Pierre?"

Pierre responded with a yawn, shrugging his shoulders.

"Mr. Whitlock, I do believe you owe us all an explanation if you know anything." Harold chastised.

"I'm afraid I must insist as well, Pierre." Emorie insisted.

"The hell are you questioning me like this for? I couldn't tell you what's going on in her head, it's not like I'm that girl's keeper." he complained.

"Dude, c'mon." Alejandro sighed.

"Pierre Mattias Whitlock, what did you do?" Gianna harped.

Darren returned back to the conversation going on around him and jumped with the amount of questioning that was occurring.

"Guys! Barking at each other won't solve anything. If he knew something about Basil, then I'm sure he'd tell us, right?"

Darren began, to which the faces on everyone soured, as though they were being somewhat sympathetic. "*Right?*"

"Haha, yeah." Pierre chuckled, giving Darren a small smile.

"Look, Darren." Gianna sighed. "You haven't been here long, so you probably don't know this manchild the way we do." she stated.

"Indeed, I'm afraid your trust in Pierre's honesty is misplaced." Emorie nodded in agreement.

"I love you guys, too." Pierre sarcastically rolled his eyes.

"Regardless..." Darren proclaimed. "...I don't think that badgering him the way you all have would do any good, and I know Basil would say the same thing if she were here right now." he affirmed. "She only spoke highly of each and every one of you, it'd hurt her to see you all not doing the same for each other." Darren finished.

"I fear the newbie speaks the truth." Gianna sighed with reluctance.

"Heh, good on you buddy." Alejandro chuckled. "You slayed the dragon."

"Dragon!?" Gianna shrieked in offense.

"How very wise, young man. Good on you for clearing the air." Harold approvingly nodded.

"Impressive work. It appears we all did lose our tempers for a moment." Emorie smiled, letting out a small sigh of relief.

Pierre remained silent, though Darren had gotten the sense that Pierre's attitude had slightly lifted, as if the pressure was relieved almost instantly. Remembering back to his time with Redmond, Darren had learned that the number one cause of a failed restaurant is a result of the imbalance of ingredients - the staff members that make up the many rich flavors of a restaurant. "Sometimes the ingredients may not mix well, but with a truly masterful chef at the helm, they soon begin to flourish." He'd speak.

"Well, it looks as though things were able to settle on their own, very good." A woman's soft voice added into the conversation.

"Chef!" The staff jumped in unison, apart from Darren, as the kitchen focused on Valeria Swifton. "It's her..." Darren thought. "The woman responsible for Redmond's death." he asserted.

"Ma'am, I didn't hear you coming in!" Emorie spoke.

"Calm down, Em, it's okay." Valeria chuckled. "I didn't want to interrupt such an enriching conversation." she explained. "Now then, we have a few topics on the agenda to discuss." she paused for a moment. "As I'm sure you're all aware, Basil is no longer with us. I know how troubling this must sound, but I received a call from her earlier today explaining that she would be returning to Maplewood." she explained.

"W-what?" Emorie jumped. "She did?"

"Yes, Emorie. I'm afraid that she was still not ready to return to the kitchen. But rest assured, I extended an open invitation to return when she was prepared."

"Unbelievable..." Darren started. "Did she *really*? How? Why?" he thought to himself in a panic.

"No fuckin way. I don't believe it." Gianna scoffed. "There's no way in hell that she'd get up and leave like that."

"...I wouldn't be too sure." Pierre grunted.

"Regardless of what we did and did not expect, let this be a lesson to you all to take your mental health seriously, and to always prioritize what's best for you and you alone." Harold preached.

"It's exactly as Harold says." Valeria nodded. "Now I too am a bit shocked by her decision, and I know better than most the implications this could have on my restaurant, but fret not, hold your heads up high."

"I-I just can't fathom her behaving like this..." Emorie said, dazed and confused.

"...You know, if any of you have something on your mind, you can always come to me, and I'll listen! Don't feel that you have to run away or something like that! We should be here for each other, especially after everything." Alejandro stated.

"Thanks, Al." Darren smiled, disheartened by Basil's departure.

"I don't accept this." Gianna interrupted. "How can you all just accept this so easily? Are you for real?"

"Gianna, I understand you're sad, we all are, but still-"

"Shut up, Emorie! You don't get it. There's something wrong going on here, Basil would never ditch us."

"Sounds like you just need to face reality, Gigi. Maybe Basil wasn't as good of a friend as you thought her to be. By the look of things, I think you need to reevaluate *a lot*." Pierre sarcastically retorted.

"Gianna, I understand you're upset, as am I, believe me. However, I do not think that lashing out is the healthiest way to go about this. Do you understand what I'm trying to tell you?" Valeria lectured.

"Yeah."

"What was that?"

"Yes...Chef." Gianna rolled her eyes.

"Now then, let's begin with the day's activities, shall we? I have much to demonstrate," Valeria segwayed.

***

Gianna was in disbelief. There was no way, she felt, that Basil would behave in such an irrational way. For as long as they've been friends, Gianna could recall just how "uptight" Basil could get, and how much of a stickler she was for the rules.

"No way in fucking hell thats changed now." she figured.

"Are you all ready for the demonstration?" Valeria asked the staff, which interrupted Gianna's chain of thoughts.

"Most certainly!" Emorie sarcastically chuckled.

"Yeah, can't wait." Gianna added on, to which Emorie let out a small grin.

Returning back to what was the most important to her, Gianna tried to brainstorm possible answers to Basil's sudden departure. "Could she have gotten really sick? Nah, I doubt it." she began to herself. "Maybe she got a better job offer somewhere else and Valeria didn't want to look bad? Mmm, nah." she continued, to no avail. "No matter how I cut it, there isn't a sound reason. What's going on?" she wondered. "Wait a minute..." she began again. "What if she's in danger?" she scared herself with the thought. "A...silhouette..." she continued. "Oh Basil, what'd you get yourself into now? I'm gonna have to knock some sense into ya when I find your sorry ass." she sighed. "If I wanna get some answers, maybe I should follow her tracks." she thought, looking around the kitchen at the different people. "Knowing her, she probably wanted to look into what she thought she saw, Basil sounded real concerned when she brought it up with me." she realized. "And that also means..." Gianna looked back on her last conversation with Heather. "...that maybe there was some truth to what she was saying. If Basil was captured by this silhouette guy, then I'm sure that Heather must know something as well." she asserted. "Right then." she concluded, returning back to Valeria's lecture.

"...and that will be all for the moment." Valeria started. "Though quick and difficult, I am confident in your abilities to replicate this dish." she declared. "When you finish with your recreation, I shall taste it for myself and see how this bodes for any potential promotion."

"...Huh?" Gianna questioned, eyes wide open.

"You have about two hours to replicate what I have shown to you all, good luck." Valeria affirmed, before clapping her hands, as the crew disbursed.

"Fucking shit." Gianna complained to herself in frenzy. "God fucking dammit." she continued.

"Do you need some help? Pierre offered, walking to Gianna as though he had done no wrong in his life.

"Fuck off, Pierre." she dismissed. "With how calm he acts, he could get away with murder, I swear it." Giana thought, walking away to a station for herself.

"Oh, hey there." Darren nervously stuttered.

"What is it!?" Gianna crudely responded, unaware of how she was coming across.

"O-oh! Sorry, I was just saying hi!"

"What's got you in such a wad?"

"W-what do you mean? Everything's fine!" Darren tried to assure her; his voice was getting higher.

"Okay then..." Gianna did not know how to carry on the conversation, and so she just pretended to start working on the recipe she knew nothing about.

There was an extended period of silence, that to Gianna felt like twenty minutes, but when she looked at the clock, it had only been two.

"...Do you by chance need help?" Darren asked.

"What was that, newbie!?" Gianna apprehensively responded, still not realizing how she's coming across.

"Oh! It's just that you looked super out of it just a while ago when the Chef was explaining her dish, and you still haven't gotten your ingredients ready, so I just assumed..."

"Well, you assumed wrong, asshole."

There was a second moment of silence, this time feeling like two hours but in reality, it had only been about a minute and fifteen seconds.

"...Well I took some notes if you want to take a loo-"

"Thank you." Gianna begrudgingly responded, snatching the small pad out of Darren's hands.

***

Harold, who had been concerned over the behavior of his peers, decided to reposition himself near Gianna and Darren. As the eldest member of the team, Harold assumed responsibility as the moral compass of the restaurant. With much experience under his belt, he knew that no other man stood as much as a little chance handling the turbulent waters of a restaurant staff - especially not one as prestigious as Val's.

It was fulfilling for Harold to see the camaraderie between Gianna and Darren, who had decided to switch notes. "That boy has a good heart...No...That MAN has a strong heart." he thought to himself. "Reminds me of a version of myself I nearly forgot about." he chuckled. In his youth, the name Harold Dunbar had an esteemed reputation that could carry itself, one Harold was exceptionally proud of. Though, one day, it all came crashing down with the release of a scathing review regarding the Maroni Factory. "That man..." he said in frustration. "He damn near ruined me! But then..."

Harold began to fade into a memory. "...She came along and saved me. And to that, I owe her everything." he smiled, looking at Valeria. "Anything she'd ask, I'd carry out with pride."

    The one thing that had been concerning Harold, however, was Basil Talbot. "I still cannot believe she would do such a thing. If only I had been able to do more...If only I had been a better mentor...a better friend even." he sighed. "Maybe Redmond was correct in his review all those years ago..." his voice trailed off. "A hindrance to the team." he sighed again. "...Hey? Harold?" a voice snapped, grabbing Harold's attention. "You okay?"

"Why yes, Mr. Perry. I appreciate the concern." he faintly smiled. "How may I assist you?"

"Well..." Alejandro began. "I was working with the fryer to try and make my own spin on the Chef's dish, and I don't think it's working properly. You think you could help me out?" Alejandro asked.

"Most certainly! And might I add, it is a very clever methodology for your dish. The future of the culinary world is saved with creatives such as yourself taking part in kitchens all over." Harold brightened up. "Now perhaps this old dog could show you some of his tricks! Haha!" he chuckled.

"Thanks man, I really appreciate it." Alejandro awkwardly laughed, walking with Harold to the fryer station.

"Now what seems to be the problem?"

"Well, you see, I was trying to drain it out to clean it, and when I went back to refill the oil, it'll only go halfway."

"Oh! Not a problem at all, I believe I know the cause of this." Harold responded. "I remember back in the day this would happen all the time, and believe it or not, I was the one getting worried that I broke something!"

"Really?" Alejandro sounded surprised. "I honestly thought of you as the man who makes no mistakes."

"A real man is able to make mistakes, identify them, and fix them as well. Always remember that young man." Harold explained. "Now, back to the fryer." Harold squatted down with slight difficulty and opened the two doors underneath the fryer, he then adjusted the pipe and turned it upward and took out the grease trap at the bottom of the fryer. "You see, sometimes, when you drain the oil from the fryer, it can get clogged up, so the best thing you can do is unscrew this piece."

Harold unscrewed a small piece from the trap. "And clean it off for a moment." he walked over to the sink and rinsed and dried it. "And then put the piece back into place. Blue to empty, red to refill. Now try it." Harold motioned, putting the fryer back into place.

    The fryer filled up normally this time with the correct amount of oil, which elicited a huge sigh of relief from Alejandro. "Thanks again man, you really saved my bacon." "Haha. Don't mention it, I'm just glad-" Harold stopped abruptly as he noticed that Alejandro was no longer paying attention to him and was on his phone, with a pained look on his face. "I-I'll be heading back now." Harold sighed, returning back to Gianna and Darren who had remained quiet the entire time.

***

Annoyed by the message he'd received, Alejandro reluctantly snuck his way over to Amore, where Marcellus had texted him to meet. "Honestly, what's the big emergency? I thought he had things handled." he complained. "At least Valeria liked my dish." he thought.

"Very well executed, Alejandro. Your drive and passion will carry you far in this industry." Valeria had praised him before they had all left Val's for the night.

"The door should be open." Alejandro recalled, reaching for the handle, which appeared to be slightly damaged. "Huh?" he questioned. "Since when-?" Forcefully tugging at the door, it finally opened. "Oh my god, what's that smell?" he shivered in disgust. The dining room was wrapped in plastic and deteriorated, as though Amore had transformed into a haunted house. "Marcellus, bro, what's your deal?" he plugged his nose. "What a shithole." he whined.

"Hello? Marcellus? It's me! What'd you want?" he yelled into the tomb, to no response. "Marcell-" his shouting was interrupted by a quick jab to his neck, as a figure injected a needle into Alejandro that knocked him unconscious.

***

After leaving Val's at around 8:30, with little to no success at recreating Valeria's dish, Gianna was exhausted. "Damn, Basil would've roasted the fuck outta me for flopping so hard." she laughed. "I'll save her." her face is growing more serious. The smell of a hot chai tea entranced Gianna and rescued her from the slump she was falling into. "Just what I needed." she sighed with relief, taking a sip.

The cafe bell rang, and a woman wearing a red beret entered, walking closer to Gianna's table. There was much reluctance radiating off Gianna, but for the sake of Basil, she figured this was a necessary evil she needed to deal with. "Better the devil you…kinda…know, I guess." she concluded, as Heather Madden took a seat across from her.

"The Blue Moon Cafe, huh? I'm very impressed."

"Oh? You know the place?" Gianna asked.

"Not this one necessarily. Back where I'm from, there's a cafe I visit with my son called the Rockefeller. This place just reminds me so much of it is all." Heather smiled.

"You have a son?" Gianna jumped in surprise.

"Haha, yes I do, he's a few years younger than you, actually."

"And where is it the two of you are from?"

"Red Moon Falls, have you ever heard of it?"

"You mean the murder capital? Serial killer safe haven?"

"The same one indeed." Heather sighed. "Though I promise it's much more than what the papers and investigators make it out to be." her voice trailed off.

Gianna was taken aback by the warmth emanating from Heather, who, up until this moment, was assumed to be just another sly and foxy reporter looking for the nearest scoop.

"I'm much more than I appear to be, Gianna." Heather laughed, "If my son knew I spilled this much information to you, I fear he'd actually strangle me." she teased. "Mom! You can't be blowing your cover like that!" he'd yell!

"...Your cover? Why are you telling me about this?"

"Well truth be told, you remind me quite a bit of my son, a little more rambunctious sure, but you both have that same headstrong attitude. I suppose I've grown quite fond of you over time." Heather elaborated.

"What is this about a cover?" Gianna asked,

"Well, you see, Heather Madden is not my real name."

Heather revealed, leaving Gianna with a look of disbelief on her face.

***

When Alejandro came to, he couldn't move, as though his entire body was glued to a chair. As he began to breathe, his heart rate increased as it was very difficult and as he shook around, he found his stomach and throat to hurt more and more. He panicked, his mouth wide open with a large tube going inside and down his throat. The sounds of something boiling filled his ears.

"Shhh. Shhh. Mm mm." a sinister voice whispered, walking out from the shadows. The figure was shrouded in chains and black clothing, with its hauntingly demonic face gazing directly into Alejandro's soul.

Trying to speak, Alejandro failed. "Shhhhhhhhhhhhhhhhhhhhhhhhhhhhhh." the Silhouette spewed. "Mm mm, mm mm!" Though Alejandro could not see their true identity, he could feel a dark and nefarious smile on the other side of the mask, a smile so transparent that it echoed through the sounds of the mocking hushes. The Silhouette pointed to his mouth and neck and shook its head.

Alejandro was unable to move any part of his body, and the more that reality set in, so did the fear and terror. No matter how hard he struggled, he couldn't free his hands and legs, and even if he could, he didn't know how he'd be able to take the tube out, which was lodged somewhere in his stomach. "W-what the fuck is going on?" he thought in fear.

The Silhouette took out what appeared to be a remote and held it up to the mask's mouth.
"It's time to think...outside the box." it spoke in an unrecognizably strained, raspy voice that sounded like a smoker.
"N-nonononononono!" Alejandro cried, only able to internally verbalize his please. "What the fuck what the fuck!?" tears rushed down his face.

The Silhouette walked over to its left and bent down, pulling the blue lever of the grease trap, which had the opposing end of the tube that was in Alejandro.
"CLEANING TIME!" the raspy voice screamed, as the boiling sounds simmered as a rush of oil ran through the tube going into Alejandro.

The oil began to pour in, and all Alejandro could feel was pain as it felt like his throat was going to explode, he couldn't breathe. More oil kept pouring in as his stomach and neck were burning. Alejandro's entire body began convulsing and shaking about as his body instinctively tried to escape from the trap he was in. His heartbeat was rushing at what felt like a hundred miles per hour. Meanwhile, as this was going on, the Silhouette took out its modified kitchen saw and swung it around the kitchen, knocking everything over, and bugs scattering. The silhouette danced around the kitchen as though it were the main attraction at a festival. Alejandro's vision was getting blurry, as all of a sudden, his stomach felt lighter and the shaking finally stopped, the sounds of dripping hitting the dirty, bug-ridden floor echoed throughout the abandoned kitchen.

 The boiling hot oil melted through Alejandro's stomach and poured out from it, his skin sizzling away and intestines falling out and plopping onto the floor like discarded ingredients, along with the oil. The banging sounds of bones hitting the floor reverberated as the plopping of intestines intensified. Alejandro's jaw ripped off as his throat began to tear open, the tube flailing on the floor as the oil ceased. "ORDER UP." The Silhouette mocked, laughing at its handywork, the saw still running in its hand.

Chapter Seven

Wrath of the Silhouette

"What do you mean your real name isn't Heather Madden?" Gianna shockingly questioned. "Who the hell are you then?" she grew weary. "What have you been doing all this time? Why have you been in Amber Creek?"

"The truth of the matter is that I am here not as a gossip reporter, but as an Investigator."

"An Investigator? Why'd you say it like that?

"I work with the Bureau of Investigations; do you recall what that entails?"

"Can't say I do, to be honest."

"Doesn't surprise me, most people commonly think that Investigators and police officers are the same thing."

"Oh, so like a private investigator?"

"Not quite, no. You see, several decades ago, back when crime around the world was at an all-time high, the police had found their hands full with a plethora of crimes - arson, terrorism - you name it. Many cases began to slip through the cracks, and many random killings, that turned out to be serial killings, were largely left undiscovered and therefore not investigated. With there being such an influx, a separate bureau was created, as a way to focus on murders. Red Moon Falls, as you are well aware, is the epicenter of most serial killings, and with police numbers running thin, a new field of investigators was created."

"How come I didn't know about this? Or anybody else for that matter?"

"Truth be told, if I had come into town with my normal hair and attire, I'm sure I'd be a lot more noticeable."

"Who are you exactly?"

"My name is Heather Caine." Heather reintroduced.

"Wait a minute, that name sounds familiar.

"I happen to have a radio show called *Life After Death*, I'm sure you've heard of it."

"...after death...after death...after death...wait a minute! H.C Holmes!?" Gianna jumped in shock, alerting other patrons of the Blue Moon Cafe.

"Shh, keep your voice down. I'm undercover, remember?"

"Oh! Right, sorry." Gianna apologized. "So what are you doing here?" she whispered.

"I received a tip that the fire that occurred at Val's a year ago was no accident, as a matter of fact, it was a cover up to a murder that took place."

"So you mean to tell me..."

"...that Redmond Thatcher was murdered? Yes. Weeks before Redmond's demise, I was made aware of a possible future crime. The sender to this day evades me, however I found it credible enough to be taken seriously. I moved into town, undercover, with the name Heather Madden and landed myself a job with a gossip magazine run by an old college pal of mine."

"This entire time...you were acting!?"

"Exactly so. I decided to team up with Marcellus, who worked alongside me and helped me blend in better as just another sleazy reporter. After the fire broke out, I too believed it was all just a terrible accident."

"Things changed with that second letter, huh? Were they both sent by the same person?" Gianna wondered.

"This could very easily be the case; however I cannot say with 100% certainty." Heather confirmed.

"How did you know you could trust me?"

"And how did you do it with me?" Heather countered.

"Instinct. Plain and simple. Sometimes, that gut feeling you get is the only thing you can trust - I've learned that many times over."

This was all a lot of information for Gianna to digest, however given the circumstances, all she could do was believe Heather. "Well my gut is telling me to trust her." she came to the conclusion. "If she were involved with whatever is going on here, I highly doubt she'd go through all this trouble. And aside from that, the lady is hella famous, no way in hell she's lyin' to me!"

"I must admit I thought I had you pegged, but I was very much wrong?"

"Pegged? What are you, some kind of pervert!?"

"I-No... That's not what I meant at all. I assumed you were a certain personality type, but that assumption I made was completely off the mark."

"How do you mean?"

"No offense, but for the last year you had behaved so headstrong and so furious, however now I can see that this was all just an illusion."

"An illusion?"

"To the real you, Gianna. You're a lot more thoughtful and inquisitive than most would suspect. You are keenly aware of your surroundings, like when you figured out that you were being followed."

"Uh...thanks I guess?" Gianna blushed, unsure as to what to say.

"Back to the matter at hand, you said you had information you wanted to share?" Heather asked.

"Yeah..." Gianna sadly sighed. "Basil brought it up to me the other night, but I shrugged it off."

"Well? What is it?"

"Basil thought she saw something the night of the fire, a silhouette is what she called it. I assured her it was Casey, but she was against that idea from the very start, insisting it was someone, or something else entirely."

"A silhouette?"

"An unsettling demon is how she described it. A shape that hid in the shadows."

"Why didn't you invite her here to talk with us? Do you have your suspicions?

"What!? No! Basil would never. At least, I don't think so." Gianna paused. "No. She wouldn't. The problem is that she's gone missing, completely skipped town according to Valeria."

"You mean the same excuse used on Casey? Seriously? From what I understood about Basil, she didn't seem like the one to just give up and quit."

"That's what I said! But Valeria said she spoke to Basil this morning."

"Did anybody else speak with her?"

"No, not at all. Everyone tried to reach out, but the voicemail box was full, and her texts stopped going through after a while. It smelled fishy from the moment Valeria brought it up."

"So two people have gone missing in the span of a few days, yeah no, something's not adding up." Heather sounded perplexed. "Valeria is definitely hiding something. But what?"

"The thing is, everyone folded so quickly and believed Valeria, except for the new guy, Darren. He's been shooting daggers at the Chef ever since we hired him."

"Darren Pierce, right? Redmond Thatcher's former protege." Heather asked for clarification.

"Basil recommended him, and to be honest, he's been doing a decent job, but still. He looked just as if not more shocked than I did."

"It sounds like we have plenty of leads to go off of, thank you for this information, Gianna. I appreciate the trust you've placed in me."

"How're we gonna go about doing this thing?"

"What do you mean?"

"You know...this..."

"Gianna, this could be too dangerous for you, there could be a potential killer on the loose and you could get hurt. I don't think..."

"Oh cut the bullshit with me, Heather. Basil was my friend, and I owe it to her to rescue her from this silhouette."

"So you believe in her testimony?"

"I didn't at first, but I'm starting now. There's just too much going on that doesn't make a lick of sense to me."

"Still, this is far too dangerous for a civilian. You should leave this to me."

"Are you serious right now, Heather? Don't you dare underestimate me for a single second! I can handle myself pretty well. I DARE some silhouette motherfucker to try it with me, I'll kill em myself!" Gianna loudly proclaimed, which disturbed the other cafe attendees.

"Gianna, calm down."

"Don't tell me to calm down! You haven't even told me all you know about this, haven't you? Do you not take me seriously!?"

"It's not that, it's just-"

"Forget about it, I knew I should've just handled this shit alone." Gianna shrugged. "Well you can't stop me. Maybe Marcellus will have more to say given he was your accomplice!" she roared.

"Gianna, no-" she walked out before Heather could finish her sentence. "...Marcellus *might* be the killer..." she said to herself, getting up from the table.

***

Heather's reluctance to disclose any information to Gianna left her feeling upset, disturbed and resentful. "The hell is her problem?" she complained to herself, parking her car. With Heather's hesitance against her, Gianna wondered if perhaps this was a pattern and that there was something missing in her that Valeria had also noticed the year prior. "I get passed up for promotion, get taken for granted by that fuck head, and now, I'm underestimated by a legendary investigator. I can't win." she said, defeated. "Did you see me like this?" Gianna continued, looking at a photo of her and Basil on her phone. Doubt began to fog her mind as she exited from her car, looking at the sign in the lot that read 'Amore'. "I'll just have to prove them all wrong." she asserted.

"I really don't want to do this." Gianna began, swallowing her pride. The last thing on the planet she wanted to do was to have to plead with Marcellus Derdrew, with whom she had a hate-hate relationship with. "I can picture it now; he'll act all high and mighty like a motherfucker and hold this information over me. Favors for years to come." she whined. When it came to Marcellus Derdrew, the two of them never clicked. Perhaps it was from a fierce loyalty towards Valeria, or perhaps it was the way he sneered and ogled over the male staff of the restaurant - regardless - he made Gianna extremely uncomfortable. "I need to do this. If Heather won't help me, I'll have to help myself."

Gianna walked to the front door, which had been blocked off by chains, and when she tried to peer inside through the glass door, the scenery was a blur, as though a filter had enshrouded the restaurant. "The hell? What's with the reno?" she questioned. "I'm surprised that he could afford something like that." she mocked.

The sounds of banging and moving around coming from the inside startled Gianna, who stepped back from the door. "Hello? You there, Marcellus?" she yelled at the door, to no response. "Hello???" she asked again to no audience. "Falling on deaf ears. Ugh." she muttered to herself, looking for another way into the building. "Well I know you're inside, so let's see if I can find another way in." She made her way to the side of the building, where a vent door laid on the ground. "It's almost like he *wants* me to come in." she commented. "Marcellus you bastard, I'm gonna give you a piece of my mind once this shit is done with." Gianna started her way in the vent leading to Amore.

The vent space was compact for Gianna, who struggled to move around in it. Unaware of where the vents would take her, she trekked forward into the darkness, with only loud noises coming from beyond her as her guide. As Gianna moved forward, her movements echoed throughout the vents. "So much for a sneaky entry."

Continuing further, Gianna stopped at the space above what she believed to be the dining room, looking down below to see if she could find where Marcellus was. Instead of finding the restaurateur, she saw a tethered figure stomping around the dining room, with their boots making a crackling noise against the plastic on the floor. Gianna breathed heavily looking down at the figure she saw strenuously working below her. She was puzzled, unsure as to what it was doing and decided to continue watching in silence. As the figure continued moving around, Gianna let out a small gasp as she saw the figure's face - a burnt and demonic look that seeped into her soul and left her feeling shattered, as though she were staring down the face of evil. "Is this...? No, it couldn't be. Oh my god." she thought to herself in a panic. "Basil was right all along." she said in disbelief. "The Silhouette..."

The Silhouette dragged a body across the small frame of view Gianna had, and in that moment, she saw the face of Casey Hope, dead and bloodied with dried blood across his cheek and neck. Dragging Casey by his feat, his neck wobbled like a bobblehead with a broken spring. Letting out a slightly louder gasp, Gianna quickly held her mouth to contain any sound as the Silhouette dragged the body away from view. She couldn't see anything more, and only heard the sounds of a chair being pulled out and a loud thud being heard. Frozen in fear, Gianna was unable to form another thought, unsure as to what move she should make next. The next moment was silent, with her feeling like she could hear a feather drop. Gianna made one large gulp with her eyes frantically analyzing the space beneath her. "What is it doing? Where did it go? She wondered. Gianna's eyes were rapidly blinking as sweat began to pour from her forehead. The only thing she could feel in this moment was dread, a feeling of overwhelming despair encapsulated her entire being. "Where's Basil!?" she internally freaked out. The room was still silent, Gianna didn't know whether she should back out or continue forward. "What the fuck do I do!?"

Before she could figure out what to do, Gianna's frenzied thoughts were startled by the sound of an engine revving in front of her. As she looked up ahead, a saw blade pierced the bottom of the vent, buzzing in a raging frenzy. "WHAT THE FUCKING HELL!?" she screamed. Looking at the blade, it began to move closer to Gianna, who, in complete fear, began to back up to try and flee through the vent's entrance. The saw continued chasing her from the front as Gianna screamed in terror. The Silhouette removed the chainsaw and aggressively walked to the back of Gianna and slashed the vent side to side, with the vent falling and causing Gianna to slide out and land on the ground. When she looked up she saw the Silhouette in full form.

"It's you! The Silhouette!" she screamed out. Gianna looked around at her at the room, as the Silhouette stood above her, staring her down to anticipate what her next move would be, the predator waiting for its prey. Across from her, at a table in the direction where the Silhouette was dragging Casey's corpse, she saw Casey propped up against a circular dining table, across from him being Alejandro, who was missing half of his body, and then next to Alejandro - Gianna screamed. "NO!" she kept muttering. "T-this can't be." she shook her head in disbelief at the sight in front of her: Basil's corpse, split nearly in two. The Silhouette looked down at Gianna, tilting its head, studying her.

When she looked at Basil's corpse, something shifted within Gianna. She stood up swiftly, to which the Silhouette jumped back - not expecting her to stand up. It was at this moment where Gianna realized that this next move would be critical, that it would decide the fate of her life. With one gulp, Gianna, whose ankle was hurting from the fall, grabbed a chair, and smashed it against the table behind her, taking two sharp pieces of wood from the remains.

"Alright motherfucker." she roared. "Let's dance." she continued. The Silhouette nodded, as though in approval of Gianna's move and revved its modified kitchen chainsaw and dragged it across the floor, before running at her. Gianna jumped to her left and avoided the Silhouette's up swing and Gianna took one of the wooden pieces and rammed it in the Silhouette's leg.

"Argh!" The Silhouette cried in pain, taking the piece out. "Now we're even." she chuckled, signaling to both of their handicaps.

Gianna backed her way up into the kitchen, which was covered in grease and blood, and which made the floor extremely slippery. "Fuck." Checking her surroundings, Gianna wobbled over to the knife rack and took out a large blade. The Silhouette stomped its way into the kitchen with the saw and used it to slash items off of the counters. "C'mon you motherfucker." she shouted. The Silhouette charged at her with perfect balance and swung the saw repeatedly and relentlessly, with Gianna unable to keep up - her arms getting sliced as she defended herself. Gianna's arms grew weak, nevertheless, she persisted and returned the Silhouettes' attacks with a swing of her knife, which the Silhouette easily dodged. "Shit. New plan." she thought, moving onto her next attack. Gianna threw the knife at the Silhouette's face, with the

Silhouette narrowly avoiding it by dropping the saw and slapping the knife away.

"Mmm Mmmm Mmmm." the Silhouette mocked, waiving its finger back and forth like a parent scolding their child. The Silhouette extended its hands out and knocked Gianna to the floor, getting down on its knees and standing on top of her. The Silhouette began choking Gianna as she struggled to keep it away, as breathing grew increasingly difficult. As she flailed and moved her hands in a struggle, Gianna grabbed the mask the Silhouette was wearing and removed it. "Y-you!" she muttered, before shutting her eyes and falling back, dead.

    The Silhouette led out a huge sigh before getting up. Turning back, they moved forward a bit, before lighting a cigarette in their coat pocket. "That was close." the Silhouette said. "That bitch almost got me. Heh." they chuckled. "And now things can proceed as they originally planned." The atmosphere of Amore's kitchen grew increasingly cold, with the cigarette's cinder acting as the sole source of heat.

    The sounds of something being grabbed off the floor missed the Silhouette's ear. All at once, the saw engine was rapidly revved, as the saw was activated, the Silhouette turned around as the saw pierced their stomach.

"This is for Basil, motherfucker." Gianna remarked.

"Ugh!" The Silhouette choked as Gianna slid the kitchen saw upward, and as blood spurted all over Gianna's face. Gianna continued to scream, as the blade continued up and slashed through their face, blood spilling everywhere like a volcano erupted. It fell to the floor on its knees and fell backward, the Silhouette's reign of terror now over.

"Gianna!" Heather screamed, entering the kitchen.

Chapter Eight

If You Could See Me Now

By the time Gianna had finished her fight against the Silhouette, she could not hear the sounds of Heather screaming her name, nor could she hear the sounds of police officers and paramedics rushing into the scene. In a state of shock, Gianna didn't feel the pain from her injured ankle or the slash wounds on her arms. A ringing sound rang in her ears, as though there had been a loud explosion, and it fractured her hearing. Covered in the Silhouettes blood, Gianna looked as though a prom prank had gone wrong. "Gianna? Hey, Gianna?" Heather repeated, trying to regain Gianna's attention. "What happened? Are you okay?" she asked, turning to the corpse on the floor. "Oh my god." she muttered.

"I-I got him, Heather." Gianna barely spoke. "The Silhouette," she began. "He's dead."

"You did a good job, Gianna, but I think we should get your wounds looked at, to make sure it's nothing too serious." Heather suggested, looking at Gianna's ankle and arms.

"W-why'd he do it?"

"We're still trying to figure it out, he didn't really indicate any signs of violence."

"But it's over, right?" to which Heather grew silent.

Heather and Gianna walked out through the dining room, where the bodies of Casey, Basil, and Alejandro were removed. Once on the outside, Valeria, Emorie, Harold, and Pierre stood in the parking lot, watching the bodies being rolled out, followed by Gianna, who was wrapped around Heather's arms.

"N-no…B-basil…" Pierre shook his head in instant regret. "W-what have I done?" tears began running down his face.

"Oh my god, how could I let this happen? I hired him, how did I not see that he…? And Alejandro…" Emorie began, sulking with frustration.

"This cannot be. Unbelievable." Harold cried.

"Despicable." Valeria grunted.

"Gianna..." Pierre tried walking up to Gianna, who was not in a state to respond to him at the moment.

"I understand you may want to speak with your companion; however the timing is very inappropriate, Mr. Whitlock." Heather began. "She needs some space."

"Since when are you...?" Pierre began. "Since when has she...?"

Heather sat with Basil in the back of an ambulance in the Amore parking lot. As she sat with her in silence, the sliced and torn body of the Silhouette, Darren Pierce, was rolled out in a body bag that wasn't fully zipped up, allowing the remaining staff of Val's to bear witness to the true face of the Silhouette.

"You're telling me the new fucking hire did this?" Pierre angrily asked. "Emorie, did you not interview him? How did you not see this coming? How could you just let Basil die!?"

"Stop acting like this is all about you, it's not like you're the only person who lost something, asshole. Don't you have a drink to drown your self-pity in?" Emorie snapped.

"Now, you both, I don't think-" Harold began.

"Shut up!" both Pierre and Emorie said.

"The two of you would be wise to listen to your senior." Valeria began, adding herself to the conversation. "Have some respect for the dead and those who still live and breathe. We lost three members of the staff, Darren excluded. Three people with whom we had developed deep bonds with."

"Well I don't know about Cas-"

"Pierre, enough. This attitude of yours will not stand." Valeria scolded. "While all of us have been idling away, ignoring the strange things happening over the course of the week, Gianna stood strong and held her ground. We may have lost those we loved, but we've gained something in return: strength. That girl has gone through hell and instead of empathizing with the poor thing, you're all just decided to make this about you. And you call yourselves chefs? Certainly not in my kitchen."

"Valeria, it's not like that. It's just-"

"Just what, Emorie, you of all people know the sacrifices we have to make, the dangers working in high profile situations bring. This pity party you're throwing for yourself will not stand."

Emorie's eyes grew wide as anger filled them. She took a step back and remained silent.

"But why would Mr. Pierce do such a thing? This doesn't make any sense to me." Harold questioned. "He and Basil were close, it doesn't add up."

"We should leave the why to the investigators. In the meantime..." Valeria took a deep breath. "...We have an opening to prepare for, and I need you all at your best."

"You cannot be serious right now." Pierre complained.

"Oh, but I am, Pierre. We can't let another tragedy overshadow all of our efforts."

"That's rich..." Emorie grumbled.

With her arms wrapped in bandages, Gianna sat with Heather on the sidewalk across the street from Val's, away from the chaos across the street.

"This is all my fault." Gianna cried.

"What? Why would you say that? How on earth could you have known?"

"Basil tried warning me about the Silhouette, and I just dismissed her and thought she was overthinking things. And now..." her voice trailed off.

"You were working with the information you had at the time; you can't beat yourself up over-"

"But I can, Heather!" Gianna interrupted, with tears streaming down her face. "I let this happen! I had a bad feeling about him when I first saw him, and I disregarded Basil's words out of my own hard headedness. I ignored ALL of the signs and just dismissed things as unimportant. I was so self-focused on working to impress Valeria, and feeling so sorry for myself for how things ended up with Pierre. I'm so fucking sorry, Heather. I treated you like shit when all you were doing was looking out for us. I ignored your pleas and went head first into the killer's den" she finished, to which Heather grabbed onto her shoulders and squeezed them. .

"Enough of this, Gianna. Look at me!" she began. "Even IF you were responsible, as you claim, which you AREN'T, the fact of the matter is that you did something about it before anybody else could! Nobody can fault you for being emotional, nobody can blame you for how you've handled life - it's been a struggle for the past year now. I understand you! What you need to remember and what I hope you can fully understand is the fact that YOU put a stop to this, not me, not Basil, not Valeria, and not any other sorry bastard! Basil died, yes, and it's a horrific tragedy, but YOU avenged her. YOU brought her killer to justice. YOU put an end to the Silhouette's wrath, okay? NOBODY else can say that."

"Heather...I..."

"Basil would not want you beating yourself up. If I knew anything about that woman it's that she deeply cared for you and your team. She went in by herself to try and save all of you, don't let her sacrifice mean nothing!"

"If only I had listened to her about what she saw the night of the fire..."

"What was that?" Heather asked again.

"What? She saw the Silhouette the night of the fire."

"Exactly..." Heather's voice trailed off for a second.

"Heather? What is it?" Gianna's voice grew strained with concern.

"Gianna, I want you to keep an open mind when I say what I'm about to, can you do that for me?"

"What is it?"

"I'm starting to realize there's more going on than just a simple killing spree." she began. "In one way or another, this has to connect to the fire from a year ago. There's no question about that. Now, let me ask you this: What do you think of the possibility that Darren was not working alone?"

"What!?" Gianna fearfully asked.

"I'm simply theorizing right now, but it makes no sense for Redmond Thatcher's protege to have killed him, not when the boy idolized him like a father. And from what Basil told you, which is something I have no reason not to believe, she saw the same Silhouette the night of the fire."

"What're you getting at?"

"The Silhouette that Basil saw started the fire, and the Silhouette you just dealt with was a separate being." Heather began scrolling through the notes on her phone. "On the night of the fire, as accounted by several witnesses and personal testimony, Darren had walked off with Alejandro - he couldn't have started the fire, even if he wanted to. He was not around the kitchen."

"Which means there has to be a second killer." Gianna asserted, this time believing Heather's words. "So what are you gonna do?"

"Well, I was hoping that you would help me." Heather began. "I want to be perfectly transparent when I tell you that I need your help on this."

"Really? You mean it?" Gianna sounded surprised.

"I have to apologize for my behavior earlier. I severely underestimated you and your abilities." Heather began. "I have to admit, my son would be giving me hell right about now for how I handled this case." she chuckled. "What do you say, are you in?"

"It'd be an honor, Heather." Gianna nodded in agreement. "No more shutting people out, no more ignoring the truth." she affirmed to herself, now with a purpose and passion that fueled her spirits.

***

Bottles were being thrown against the wall, shattering on impact. A table full of cans, frames, plates, and other miscellaneous items were being swung off the table and onto the floor - the apartment space looking like a garbage dump.

"Fuck!" Pierre screamed, dropping to the floor in defeat. A landslide of emotions overtook him, as he looked down to the floor withering away in his own self-pity. Guilt was amongst the strongest feelings that enshrouded his mind. With the discovery of Darren Pierce's murderous rampage, Pierre couldn't help but feel as though he was somehow culpable. "W-what's wrong with me?" he cried, looking at the empty bottles and mess that surrounded him.

 The past few days had been a blur to Pierre, who had been drunk or on some other type of substance the entirety of the time. When he believed that Basil stood him up, the feelings of resentment he had been harboring only continued to fester. "I never got the chance to tell her." he sighed in defeat. "AHHH" he screamed into the void. "What'd I do…?" his voice trailed off. "I should've been there for her, but instead…" he threw another bottle by his feet towards the wall. "FUCK." he yelled. "What do I do now?"

 Pierre felt defeated, no longer wanting to go to work, no longer wanting to see any of his old coworkers, and no longer wanting to live. Everything in Pierre's life was falling apart before him, with those he cared about dying and with the life he had grown accustomed to changing ever so rapidly. Pierre hated this change. Thinking back to the year before,

Pierre's life was going great - he had a girlfriend who worshiped him and a job that any man would dream of. With all taken into consideration, there were still parts of Pierre that wanted more, needed more. When he had first met Basil, Pierre initially had given her no time of day as she ignored all of his antics. However, the more they began working alongside each other, the more Pierre began to realize that there were feelings brewing between them. Perhaps it was the thrill of the hunt, or maybe even Basil's romantic disinterest, regardless, Basil soon became the center of all of Pierre's thoughts. "I wonder if she ever knew…" he thought to himself, shaking his head. "No…" he concluded. "She wouldn't have left me. No way in fucking hell." he affirmed. "Still…I'll never get to see her again." he cried.

  Pierre picked up one of the picture frames he knocked on the floor that was a group photo of the entire staff of Val's. "We all looked so happy here," he began. "But now…" Pierre looked at Gianna in the picture, which evoked feelings of intense remorse and grief. "And where do I begin? With the way I've treated Basil…treated Gigi…" he set the frame down on the table and stood up. "I can't afford to waste another moment." he started. "I ruined everything." He wiped tears from his eyes. "And now, I need to fix what I've broken." Pierre stated aloud, with a strong sense of determination. "Right. It's better late than never, I guess." he said, walking towards his fridge and grabbing the drinks out of it. Pierre grabbed a garbage bag and threw the bottles in and went around the apartment to clean the mess of space.

***

The sounds of milk being steamed and the aroma of coffee beans filled the room with an overwhelming sense of coziness. Despite the crowded space, Harold found solace within the confines of the Blue Moon Cafe.

"You know, I would meet here with Basil every Saturday morning for a coffee and pastry." Harold reminisced, taking a bite of his chocolate muffin.

"Is that so?" Emorie asked, following the conversation.

"It was here where she proclaimed that one day she too would have her own establishment," he recalled. "It's a shame, really." he shook his head.

"She had what she wanted down in Maplewood, a part of me doesn't understand why she would want to come back." Emorie pointed out, taking a sip from her latte.

"Well the same could be said about you, Ms. Wallace." Harold added. "You've been able to make a name for yourself, why'd you come back?"

"I guess there was still a part of me that had something to prove." Emorie figured.

"And the same with Basil, too. And with me as well. It seems likely that we all felt that our work from one year ago never got the true resolution it deserved." Harold took another bite from his muffin.

"But still, it doesn't feel right. You know, with the way things have turned out."

"Life often never goes the way we plan it, no matter how hard one may try." Harold took a large gulp of his hot chocolate. "That being said, I fully agree with you." he sighed. "Those three did not deserve the fates they ended up with. Hell, even Mr. Hope deserved better."

"Didn't you hate the guy?"

"Hate is a very strong word. I'd rather say I had no respect for the boy. He never acted his age and always treated his elders with disrespect. And when he got the promotion last year..."

"...You didn't agree with it either, huh?"

"I was appalled, fully taken aback by Valeria's decision. I was certain Basil would be selected."

"I'll drink to that." Emorie agreed, taking another sip from her drink. "For certain this time." she added.

"What was that?"

"Well, Valeria was going to promote Basil, she told me so. Now, a lot of what that woman says is untrustworthy, however that much I was sure about. Dammit!" Emorie took a deep breath. "This isn't fair, none of it is."

"Is there something lingering in your mind, Ms. Wallace?

"I feel like there was some merit to what Pierre was saying, like part of this was all my fault."

"You can't listen to a word that drunken fool says, he was talking out of his ass."

"It's easy enough for you to say that when you don't have the guilt of hiring a killer hanging over your neck, Harold. Valeria trusted my instincts and that in itself cursed me. I trusted my gut and look where it led us: three dead bodies."

"But Ms. Wallace, one cannot be certain that Mr. Pierce would have not gone on the offensive regardless. There's no way of guaranteeing what you did had any factor as to what he would do. You understand as much, right?"

"I suppose so. Be that as it may, nobody deserved to die."

"With that we are in agreement. I wish there was more I could've done as well. Perhaps if I had been more inquisitive with Basil, then maybe I could've saved her."

"You know how she is, always prodding where she doesn't need to. That girl had a knack for getting herself into trouble." Emorie added.

"Oh believe me, I know good and well. When I was her teacher, she would always look for out of the box methods to counter my traditional techniques. I would always catch her spying on me as I made dishes, or talking to other chefs about their secret tricks, even when I explicitly told her not to."

"Did she get in trouble for that?" Emorie chuckled.

"Every single time." Harold laughed. "There would be moments where I would catch her using an unorthodox cooking method I prohibited her from using. She would finish dishes earlier than it should normally take, and she'd just insist she was that good!"

"And how'd that go for her?"

"As well as you'd expect! You may be able to fool the eyes, but never the tongue! Haha! And when I would call her out on it, she would say 'But Harold, it still turned out good!'." Harold took the last sip of his hot chocolate. "Sometimes, tradition is key."

"What a tall difference from the chef she turned out to be! Looking at her skills now, I would never have assumed she was so...experimental...with her cooking!" Emorie said in amusement.

"It was mighty exceptional to see the person she was becoming. It's a damn shame that..." Harold's voice trailed off once more, as he stared into the reflection of the glass mug.

"You know, to lose Basil was bad enough, but Alejandro as well..." Emorie started "It felt like somebody pierced my heart, as though a part of me died with him."

"You two were close, weren't you?"

"He was my knight." Emorie tearfully chuckled. "That man would have gone to hell and back for me."

"I never saw how close you two had grown."

"We tried to keep our personal lives outside our professional ones, for the sake of the restaurant and our sanity." she shook her head. "And besides…that harpy would've dug her talons into him if she had known…" she grumbled, to which Harold didn't hear.

"I've always thought that work and personal lives should remain separate. Never mix the two, as it's only a recipe for disaster."

"It pisses me off that an outsider just came and ripped our work family apart, like some mad doctor." Emorie spoke up in frustration.

"What I don't understand is the *why* of it all."

"That monster must've had his fair share of problems. I can only hope investigators are able to give us the answers we need." Emorie asserted.

"And that investigator, Heather Madden, I was shocked to find out that she is the real H.C Holmes." Harold pointed out.

"I never knew she was so close to Ms. McKnight."

"News to me too. I never pegged Gianna as one to cozy up with investigators. But I'm sure this investigation will be in good hands with her on the case. I wonder what brought her into town."

"I'm sure we could always ask her." Harold figured.

"I'm certain this won't be the last we see of her." Emorie added.

"What makes you say that?"

"A hunch." Emorie responded. "Someone as famous as her is surely a meticulous and thorough person, I'm sure she'll be coming around to ask us an array of questions."

The conversation grew silent for an abrupt moment as both Harold and Emorie took the time to collect their thoughts.

"Hey, Harold?"

"Yes, Ms. Wallace?"

"Let's do our best to make them proud, so that way when they look to us from wherever their spirits go, they can be proud."

"A most excellent suggestion, Ms. Wallace."

"You know you can just call me Emorie, right? We've worked with each other for quite a while now, there's no need to remain so formal."

"You're right." Harold chuckled. "I suppose I can do that. After all, it's not like we're unfamiliar with each other. Let's aim for the top, Emorie." he smiled.

***

Heather never foresaw herself collaborating with a staff member of Valeria Swifton's restaurant, let alone Gianna McKnight. If anything, she thought, it would've been Basil Talbot, the promising chef and baker from Maplewood. Regardless of how things ended up, there were parts of Heather that felt glad she had the opportunity to work with Gianna. Even from her time undercover the year prior, there was always a part of her that held high disdain towards Marcellus and the way he treated the young girl. That being said, she couldn't just up and go against him either, as that would've jeopardized her position. "Though that may make me a bad person..." Heather thought. "...sometimes you have to play the role of villain to get the justice you seek." she firmly believed.

Heather began her investigation of Valeria Swifton a year prior, having received an anonymous tip that a violent crime would occur at Val's. Knowing good and well that a menacing note such as that could've just as easily been a prank, Heather couldn't ignore the possibility that it was very real. "My gut is telling me to believe this." she recalled. Heather realized that if she went to the police or her fellow investigators for assistance, that could very well mean more danger for those involved at Val's. What didn't help was when Heather's youngest son, Elias, had discovered the letter as well.

"Mom, you're going to check on this, right?" he asked.

"Eli! What did I say about going through my things?" she returned, trying to dodge the question and put the focus back on him.

"I know what you're doing, H.C." he responded, immediately catching on to what she was doing. "Well? Are you gonna do something about this? *Right?*"

"But it might not be anything at all. And besides, I'd hate to leave you again."

"And what if it *is* something? You're THE Heather Caine! You're not one of the best for nothing! Besides, I can fill your shoes in Red Moon Falls while you're away! I'm your son after all!" he cheered.

    When it came to her investigative prowess, Heather always had the talent for uncovering truths hidden behind layers upon layers of lies. It was this innate talent that gave her the nickname "H.C Holmes." As she talked to Eli about her cases, the more she began to realize that he too had inherited her gift. "My sweet boy, what am I going to do with you?" she smiled, looking adoringly at her son.

"Well, you got me again, Eli. Heh." she chuckled. Eli had always been her weakness, the one person she could never say no to.

"Alright! You're the best! I knew you would!" Eli applauded.

"Now go kick some ass and save some lives!"

"In that order?"

"Well..."

    The sound of Gianna's voice brought Heather back to the present, sitting in Gianna's living room.

"You good?" Gianna asked, as Heather came to.

"Apologies, lost in thought." she explained.

"If you say so, H.C."

"So where are we on suspects?" Heather stood up and looked at the whiteboard in front of them. On the board, were the names and pictures of those who have survived thus far, with a picture of Darren on the opposing bottom side, with the word killer underneath and a large question mark to the right of his photo, with the word accomplice written underneath.

"Well, we have the most obvious suspect, Marcellus Derdrew." Gianna began, tapping the marker against his picture. "Both Darren and the bodies of Casey, Basil, and Alejandro were discovered at Amore, as though the restaurant was being used as the Silhouette's nest."

"I've been skeptical about Marcellus from the beginning. It would make sense for him to have sent the invite and then work with me, that way he could frame the fire and the bodies as bad press for Valeria."

"Exactly. If he had THE H.C Holmes on his side, then he could ruin Valeria's career." Gianna nodded in agreement.

"What about Emorie Wallace? Harold Dunbar? Emorie has grown to become a rising star in the culinary world, it's possible she wanted to destroy Valeria's career to uplift her own. And Harold had previous experiences with Redmond, did he kill him out of revenge and then use the cover of a fire to hide his tracks?

"Emorie doesn't really strike me as the opportunist type, if I'm honest. She's been nothing but kind to all of us and was in a relationship with Alejandro. With the way those two cared for each other, I highly doubt she'd harm him."

"They were dating!? Really?"

"Yeah, they kept it hidden but most of us knew about it the whole time." Gianna explained. "Harold is too much of a hard ass to intentionally do something that would halt his career, I don't think there's a man as obsessed with the kitchen as him." she paused for a moment. "What about Valeria?"

"You think Valeria Swifton could be behind all of this?" Heather asked. "I'm impressed, you're starting to think like a real investigator."

"Heh, you really think so?"

"An investigator has to be able to examine all angles, regardless of how small. Otherwise, their web of deduction will be nothing more than a scrambled mess. And Valeria would in a way make some sense. Here." Heather handed Gianna a note.

"What's this?" Gianna paused to read the note. "Oh my god! Is this?"

"Redmond Thatcher's notes of Val's. Marcellus had this locked away in his desk drawer."

"Bland food...less than appealing plating...good waiting staff...an imbalance in the kitchen...my god, he was going to write a bad review!"

"Precisely! There's a very real possibility that Valeria silenced Redmond before he could publish his review, knowing how damaging it would be to her."

"But what if someone else on staff knew about this review? It'd damage any one of us." Gianna pointed out.

"Now, I know you may not want to think about this..." Heather began. "But..."

"But what?"

"Pierre Whitlock?"

"N-no."

"No?"

"No."

"Gianna, we need to talk this through. I understand you and him have a very long...and rather complex history, however we need to examine -"

"Every angle, yeah, I remember what you said. I just have a hard time believing he could do something like this. Especially with his busted ankle."

"How did he hurt his ankle?"

"A fight with Casey."

"So you mean to tell me he had issues with Casey Hope?"

"Yeah, but the asshole tormented him every chance he got."

"Which could be the motive for Casey's murder. And with the shouting match he had with Basil, there's motive, albeit a loose one, for her murder as well." Heather suggested.

"He wouldn't have killed Basil. I know that much for a fact."

"How do you know for certain?"

"...I really gotta say it out loud, don't I?"

"Gianna? What do you mean? What are you talking about?"

     Gianna paused for a moment as the conversation stalled, similar to a western style showdown. She took a deep breath in and then out, looking down to the floor.

"...He loved her." Gianna looked back up at Heather with tears in her eyes.

"He what!?"

"I don't really know when it started, but for the longest time, Pierre has had a huge crush on Basil, though the girl was too clueless to ever catch on." She sat down. "The way he'd look at her and give her his attention...There's no doubt."

"Gianna, I didn't know-"

"I guess that just makes me the other woman I guess?" she sadly chuckled. "I accused him of hurting Basil knowing good and well he'd never lay a finger on her. I just didn't want to accept the fact that the man that I loved..."

"Gianna..."

"And you know what? I spent the last year taking care of him, watching over to make sure he didn't die from all the alcohol he drank. I thought to myself, 'you know what? Maybe, just maybe, if I give him more attention and show him that I care, that he'll fall back in love with me. That the Pierre who I made so many happy memories with would come back.' But he didn't. The moment she came back, the lustful gaze in his eyes returned."

Heather felt an immense sense of grief for Gianna, whose tears started falling down her face at a much faster rate. "Oh Gianna..." Heather thought, unsure of how to proceed. "This has been a horrible experience for her all around. It's finally all hit her."

"Fuck him." Heather blurted out, unintentionally thinking out loud.

"What was that?" Gianna looked up, wiping the tears off her face.

"Dammit! Not what I meant to say!" Heather thought to herself. "It's clear he didn't deserve you to begin with. You are more than he could ever hope to find." Heather nodded. "Don't sacrifice your own sanity for the sake of another, especially not a man. *Especially* not Pierre of all people. I may not know you all too well, but I've seen enough to know that you are more than he could ever handle. The man can't even handle himself without a goddamn bottle. Gianna, you're a very strong-willed woman, meanwhile he's a no willed leech. You battled a serial killer, and what did he do? Battle a bottle? Bitch please, give me a break." Heather finished, to which Gianna chuckled.

"You sure do have a way with words." Gianna started to smile, the defeat in her voice disappearing. "You're right. I need to let him go."

"Now that's what I want to hear!" Heather cheered, ripping Pierre's picture off of the list. She turned and looked at the clock, which read 8:30 P.M. "Why don't we take a break for a moment and get a pizza? My treat." she suggested.

"I'd like the sound of that." Gianna nodded in agreement.

Heather knew that in hard times it was important to reserve small slots to enjoy the little things, and to decompress. With the soft opening imminent, Heather knew that soon enough the second Silhouette would strike, and she and Gianna would need to be ready for whoever it may be. "Soon." Heather thought. "We'll bring this son of a bitch to justice"

Chapter Nine

Ashes to Ashes

The atmosphere of Val's felt akin to a haunted graveyard, filled with the spirits of those long departed. There was something dreadful about having to proceed with work mere hours after discovering that your coworkers were brutally murdered. The energy at Val's was sunken deep like a ship at the bottom of the ocean, bound for an eternal abyss. The flames that stoked the hearts of the once eager chefs had diminished into a tiny, faint spark.

Gianna was still shaken up by the day before, walking with a touch of apprehensiveness in her step. It felt cruel to have to work past the enduring trauma, however Gianna knew that she needed to remain at the soft opening. Had it not been for Heather, Gianna was unsure as to whether she would've stuck around or fled town. "There's a second bastard, and he's bound to show up tonight." she remembered. Darren's death had to have put a dent in whatever scheme the Silhouette had conjured up, and the soft opening would be the perfect opportunity to act." Amongst the guests arriving for the night, there were food critics and friends of Valeria, alongside other respected members of the Amber Creek community. To ensure a successful and lively night, Valeria ensured that attendance levels would be high. To Gianna, this felt miserable, a restaurant full of high-profile clientele being served by a mere two servers - both her and Pierre. "We're understaffed and underprepared." she grumbled.

"Chin up, Gianna." Emorie sat next to Gianna in the dining room. "Trust me when I say you're not the only one pissed off right now, pardon my language." she shook her head. "Given all that's happened, she should've closed the doors, at least temporarily."

"You're telling me, this is actually ridiculous! I mean, seriously, half our staff got butchered by some psycho maniac freak, and her first instinct is to stick with the reopening?"

"There has to be something more to it." Emorie felt. "It's like she knew this is how things would turn out, and it's like she's fully confident that the opening will go smoothly. It terrifies me that she could act so cold. Basil...Alejandro...Ugh! This feels disrespectful to their memory!"

"I would share the same sentiment." Harold added, walking into the restaurant. "Apologies for the tardiness, there were a few things I needed to take care of." he explained, taking a seat. "It feels emptier." he sighed.

"...A ghost town." Pierre commented to himself, walking into the restaurant with an expression of disdain on his face.

"Well look who the cat dragged in. I'm glad you showed up, Pierre." Emorie greeted.

"Mr. Whitlock." Harold abruptly responded.

Gianna jumped a bit, unsure of how to navigate a discussion with Pierre. The look on Pierre today was different from the last few days, the last few years even. "He looks...sorta cleaned up?" Gianna was surprised.

"Hey, Gigi." Pierre awkwardly greeted. "Mind if I sit here?" he signaled to the seat next to Gianna.

"...I guess." she mumbled as Pierre sat down.

"Listen, you guys. There's something I feel the need to tell you--" Pierre began, before being interrupted by another voice.

"I'm pleased everyone is finally here." Valeria's powerful voice echoed from the back of the room, walking closer into the light being cast down from the glass ceiling.

"...never mind I guess." Pierre reacted silently.

Gianna kept her gaze fixed on Valeria, hoping to pick up any clues that she might have some sort of involvement with the Silhouette. Given what she knew about Valeria, the idea that she could potentially be the killer sent a chill down her spine. However, this same chill kept Gianna on high alert, ready to pounce at any given second.

"You all look so...grim." Valeria sighed. "This won't do."

"Well Valeria, our friends are dead, do you expect a celebration?" Pierre barked back, to which the rest of the team gasped.

"What was that, Pierre?" her left eye twitched.

Pierre was growing tired of the disrespect he and his team had endured through Valeria's managerial methods. Though his mind remained somewhat foggy, he grew increasingly frustrated over Valeria's sudden willingness to just move on and act as though nothing happened. "If I can't apologize, I must atone." he felt, reflecting upon his behavior since the week began. Pierre stood up.

"You're being disrespectful!" Pierre accused, to which Emorie let out a small grin and Harold simply shook his head in disdain.

"Pierre!" Gianna scolded. "Are you drunk!? Seriously!?"

"Nah, Gigi, not this time." he responded. "I may not be in the healthiest state at the moment, but I'm still sound enough to know disrespect and abuse when I see it." he continued.

"You!" he pointed to Valeria. "You've fostered an environment of competition and distrust and look where that's gotten all of us! Half of us are dead! Murdered! And you're only response is to keep fucking moving forward like a blind ass fucking solider marching to their fucking death!"

"Is that so, Pierre?" Valeria asked, without blinking and staring daggers in Pierre's direction.

"Pierre, stop!" Gianna pleaded.

"No, Pierre, keep going, I must insist." Valeria demanded.

"I'm done with your bullshit Valeria. You're just as responsible for this chaos as Darren fucking Pierce, you scaly bitch!"

"...and he said it." Emorie said to herself.

"Oh my..." Harold sighed.

"Pierre..." Gianna looked concerned.

"You know Pierre, unlike you, some of us unfortunately have to act like adults. I'm sorry that the opportunities I generously provided you with did not meet your expectations. I'm sorry you're misplacing the blame for the failure as a chef and human being that you truly are onto me. Well, grow the fuck up you manchild. All I've done for you; all I've done for ALL of you is be supportive and uplifting! When I lost MY restaurant so very tragically, who was it that offered to rescue you from the depths of your despair? Who is the one GIVING you a career with a golden fucking spoon? Was it Basil? Was it Alejando? Was it fucking Casey?"

"You'd know a lot about fucking Casey, wouldn't you?" Pierre clapped back, which created an expression of absolute hate on Valeria's face. "Oh? Did I strike a sore spot? Awwwwwww."

"Get her, Pierre." Emorie silently cheered. "Get her again!"

"After all I've done, this is how you treat me." she responded. "I'd highly recommend you keep your mouth closed unless you would like a lawsuit slapping you across the face." Valeria threatened.

"Is that all you got, bitch?" Pierre responded.

"You know Gianna, you should consider yourself lucky. I woke up this morning planning to fire you for betraying us and working with Heather Caine, but you're in luck because Pierre: you are fired!" she screamed.

"What?" Gianna gasped.

"You were going to do what now?" Harold gagged.

"You cannot be serious..." Emorie added.

"Get the hell out of my restaurant you son of a bitch, before I make you!" Valeria demanded.

"Threatening me, good look, seriously!" Pierre sarcastically smirked. "Then I'm outta here, may you burn just like your old shithole of a restaurant did." he finished, getting up and preparing to leave, before Gianna grabbed his arm.

"Why did you-?"

"The writing was on the wall," he began. "Good luck, Gigi." Pierre smiled before walking away. "...and thank you, for everything, Gianna." he said under his breath. "Catch ya later everyone." he waved goodbye, leaving Val's.

"Reconvene here an hour before opening, we'll all talk then." Valeria commanded, before aggressively turning around and returning to the kitchen.

***

Unaware of the events that transpired hours before she arrived, Heather was left pondering as to why Val's felt so empty. For Heather, this emptiness was a golden opportunity to investigate the restaurant. "We're in the endgame, it's now or never." she justified, walking towards the kitchen. As she walked through the dining room, Heather could've sworn that she heard a beeping noise but was unsure if that was just the restaurant equipment. The sounds of footsteps and door shutting could be heard in the distance, grabbing Heather's attention. Heather assumed that it was the last of the staff leaving the building, and so she continued forth.

The kitchen itself was meticulously cleaned out, with the new kitchen equipment shining from the bright lights. "Impressive work, Valeria. I wonder how one procures such a budget to create a kitchen space as grand as this." she questioned. The walk-in freezer was left open as gusts of cold air blew through the kitchen. "Too reckless for your own good I fear." she commented. "Something's wrong." she spoke aloud. Heather's suspicions were raised as she looked around the kitchen, avoiding the walk-in freezer. "There's no way, it's a trap." she suspected, as she continued surveillance. Heather moved towards Valeria's office.

    Rummaging through her papers, Heather noticed that Valeria's recipe cards were in a different form of handwriting than the rest of Valeria's work. "Wait a minute…" she was interrupted.

"I should've figured a rat like you would scurry around a kitchen. On brand when you think about it." Valeria insulted, from behind Heather, across the kitchen, hands behind her back.

"So you knew I'd be here." Heather responded, dropping the papers in her hand onto the desk.

"You're not the only intellect in town, H.C Holmes. I figured that Gianna showing her face here after what she did to me told me all I needed to know. You really can't let things go, can you?" Valeria walked closer.

"Not when I'm close to the truth, Ms. Swifton. Or do you prefer chef? I hear about how temperamental you can get." Heather exited the office, now in closer range to Valeria.

"Is that so?" Valeria grinded her teeth.

When Heather turned around, Valeria was right behind her and from behind her back, Valeria pierced Heather with a corkscrew.

"Apologies, you know how temperamental I can get." she smiled, as though there was a mixture of pure joy and malice behind her face. "Now only if you could learn to stay out of people's business. Tsk. Tsk. I expected more from you." she shook her head, twisting the screw further into Heather.

"Wh-wha-"

"Shhh. Shhh." Valeria put a finger to Heather's mouth. "I'm tired of your voice." her smile turned to an expression of disgust. "I can't have you ruining the night for me, now can I?" Valeria, with the screw still in Heather, pushed her into the walk in and closed the door, locking it from the outside. "I think you should cool off a little." Valeria chuckled, turning her back to the door.

Heather, in the walk in, began shivering and grunting from the pain of the stab wound. She stared up at the light in the walk in, feeling dizzy and in pain. "It can't end like this, I need to-" Heather stood up to try for the door. As she stood, her position grew wobbly as she stumbled back onto the floor, her vision fading to black, with the last thing she could see were several boxes with timers and wires sticking out of them, laying underneath the bottom of the food shelves, and the last thing she could hear was more of that beeping.

***

Emorie walked across the street to Amore with feelings of grief cursing her heart. Even with the caution tape wrapping the building, there was still part of her that felt unsafe. "What a busy afternoon. This whole thing has been awful, really." she sighed in defeat. "Everything I've set out to do has seemingly crumbled before my very feet. Alejandro…" her voice trailed off. "Here I thought I was better at controlling my emotions, heh." she tearfully laughed. "C'mon, Emorie, you're better than this." She tried to boost her confidence back up. "There's still work to do."

Despite making a name for herself, a part of Emorie felt incomplete, as if the accolades she had acquired over the past year have meant nothing. "All they do is ask me about Valeria." she shook her head. "No. I need to make a name for myself. Start doing things for me." she finished, weighing her options. "Maybe I should leave." she began to realize. "And based on what happened earlier..." she started. "...her approval doesn't mean much to me anymore. Time to move on." she began.

The energy surrounding Amore left Emorie feeling scared, though she felt she needed to get a good look at the place, to regain control over her emotions and to hopefully obtain the closure she desired. A mysterious hand suddenly and abruptly reached out from behind Emorie. "What!?" she gasped, before a pressure hit her neck and she fell to the floor.

***

Harold disappeared after the argument between Valeria and Pierre. And even then, Gianna grew increasingly worried as her thoughts continued to focus on Pierre. "Why did he do that?" she wondered to herself, feeling anxious. "That asshole's gonna have to explain himself." she continued. "Stupid. Stupid. Stupid!" she groaned.

Gianna didn't feel comfortable staying at Val's, and the thoughts of staying in that area left her with feelings of worry. There was a growing discomfort in her chest, a nervousness that rushed throughout her bloodstream as she continued her vigilance wherever she went. "There's no telling..." she began, recalling her experience at the market. "Dammit! I hate this, I feel so weak! UGH!"

Looking at the clock, Gianna knew she had to make her way back to Val's and reconvene with the staff. "Where's Heather? I haven't heard back from her." she pondered, looking at the seemingly endless stream of messages she sent to Heather. Leaving Blue Moon Cafe, Gianna made her way back to Val's, still in disbelief over Pierre's behavior. "I cannot let this bastard distract me, never again!" she tried to shrug it off. "But what would Basil do?" she asked herself, unsure of what she was doing. "Dammit! If only she were still here, if only it was me instead of her-" she cut herself off. "But she wouldn't want that, would she?" she proceeded, reflecting on Heather's words. "I'll do this for you." she affirmed.

The closer she got to Val's, the stronger the feeling of dread turning knots in her stomach grew. "And to my grave I go." she said, entering the parking lot. "Looks like everyone else is already here." Gianna commented, looking at her co-workers' cars. "That's strange." Gianna noticed that Heather's car was also parked in the lot. "If she's here, why hasn't she responded to any of my texts?" she began to ask herself.

The atmosphere inside Val's was grim, with there being no sight of another person. To Gianna, this was suspicious and her worry over the night only continued to grow.
"Hello?" Gianna yelled, her voice echoing throughout the dining room. "Anyone there?" she asked aloud, to no response.

Gianna's heart sank as the feeling of worry that had been brewing began to manifest itself.

She looked around in a panic as the sounds of footsteps scurrying across the floor and beeping noises flooded her ears. "Hello!?" she asked again, refusing to budge from her spot in the dining room. "Nope. If I explore, I'll die." she guessed. "Aint gonna happen."
"Gianna?" a concerned voice cried out, coming out from the kitchen. "My god, I'm glad you're here, I haven't been able to

get a hold of anyone!" Valeria explained. "Do you know what's going on?" she asked, her hands behind her back.

"I don't know, you tell me, Valeria." Gianna asked with a suspicious tone. "The hell is she doing here? She looks guilty as fuck." she thought.

"Oh not you too." Valeria complained.

"Where is everyone? Their cars are here."

"I just assumed everyone went for a walk." Valeria responded, walking up to an apprehensive Gianna.

"And what about Heather?" Gianna interrogated, with Valeria raising an eyebrow."

"Heather? What about her?"

"Her car is here too, Valeria. What's going on?" Gianna asked, taking a step back, Valeria following suit.

"Gianna, if I didn't know any better, I'd think you didn't trust me!" Valeria giggled. "What's wrong? Come closer, Gianna." she smiled.

"N-nah. I'm good."

"Now, Gianna..." Valeria began. "We're a team, we need to trus-" her voice abruptly cut off as she coughed up blood.

"Ack!" she choked. "Agh!" she screamed as a knife pierced her back for the second time. "Y-you've got to be kidding me." Valeria fell to the floor, with a puddle of blood beginning to form around her.

From behind Valeria, stood a rattled Marcellus Derdrew, whose bloodied hands were shaking.

"M-marcellus?" Gianna gasped, with tears running down her face.

"S-she's dead! Don't worry about it!" He responded, with a knife in one hand and a folder in another. "Don't worry, I stopped her!" he nervously laughed.

Gianna took a step back.

"G-gianna, you don't have to be scared anymore! Valeria's dead!"

"Marcellus, what the fuck did you do!?" Gianna screamed.

"Why are you yelling!?" he asked. "I said...she's dead! It's okay!"

"What the fucking fuck man!?" she screamed, shaking her teary head, backing up some more.

"Listen, I know how this might look, but I swear I'm doing what's right! Look, I'll admit I planned on sabotaging Valeria's opening, but I swear I didn't kill anyone Gianna, you have to trust me!" Marcellus stressed with the knife in his hand. Noticing the fear in Gianna's eyes, and looking back at the knife in his hand, Marcellus dropped it. "Oh! I'm sorry." he began. "I don't mean to scare you, I swear. I was locked in the trunk of Valeria's car for the last twelve hours; she knew what I was planning on doing and tried to stop me. She killed all of your friends! I saw the masked man in my restaurant, he's the one that put me in her trunk!" Marcellus tried to explain. "Here!" Marcellus held his hands out, signaling Gianna to grab the folder. "Take a look for yourself."

"What is that?"

"Proof! Proof that Valeria's whole career has been a LIE. Proof that Valeria has been holding onto A LOT of secrets! Here!"

Before Gianna could walk over, the sound of an electric motor revved up as a modified kitchen saw sliced Marcellus' arms off, the folder and its contents flying everywhere. The source of the saw came from a face all too familiar to Gianna - the Silhouette.

"AHHHH!!" Marcellus screamed holding what remained of his arms up in front of him.

The Silhouette chipped away at his arms like a butcher chopping up meat. It proceeded to rapidly slice Marcellus side to side starting up from his head and making its way down to his knees. All Gianna could do was drop to the floor and cover her mouth with her hands, paralyzed by fear. When the Silhouette finished, Marcellus' body collapsed to the floor in several different pieces. A picture from the envelope revealing a lude photo of Casey having sex with Valeria in her office landed by Gianna's feet.

"Fucking dammit!" the familiar voice of the Silhouette complained, taking off its mask.

Chapter Ten

The Main Corpse

"Well? Does it surprise you, Gianna? To see me as the face behind the mask you fear so much. Or, perhaps, this comes as no shock to you? Tell me, which is it?"

The only sound breaking the silence was that of beeping. There was a traffic jam of emotion driving through Gianna's mind as she shakily stood mere feet before the true face of the Silhouette. To the question before her: yes. The more Gianna began to think about it, the more she realized that there wasn't much she knew about the killer before her, that the coworker she had spent so long with was an enigma that never had much space in her mind. Regardless of that fact, there she stood, face to face with the Silhouette. Gianna pressed the button of a device in her back pant pocket.

"I believe this may be the first time I've truly seen you speechless! Though, your face tells me everything I need to know."

For once, Gianna was at a loss for words, as though the perfect combination of phrases to help capture the feelings and thoughts flowing through her had escaped. The number of questions that pop upkeep multiplying the more Gianna continues to dwell on the situation before her. "What do I do?" she wondered, unsure of what her next move could be.
"Well? Say something, Gianna." the Silhouette demanded.
"I... I really don't know how to respond to you, Emorie."
"Is that so?" Emorie chuckled. "I guess I could just get things over with before, well, you know..." Emorie stopped to make a boom noise. "The big bang!" she laughed. "Kaboom!"
"What do you mean Emorie, what are you talking about?" Gianna panicked.
"Don't tell me, you haven't been hearing all that beeping?" Emorie rolled her eyes.
"Beeping!?" Gianna focused her hearing to the ticking noises that had been passively ringing throughout the restaurant.
"I failed one year ago to destroy Valeria, I'm afraid I cannot

make the same mistake twice, it would simply be disgraceful. An utter failure. A stain on the memories of those whose lives have been lost, may they rest in peace." Emorie said, as though it were painful for her to reminisce on those who she had killed. "A tragedy, really." she sighed. "So, this time, I'm leaving no room for failure. In approximately thirty minutes, this restaurant shall fall to the flame!"

"Emorie, you sick motherfucker." Gianna said with disgust, "How could you!? You killed your friends, your coworkers..."

"My friends? Gianna let's not fool ourselves. I knew you were an easy whore, but a stupid one too. Color me impressed with your range."

"A whore? Fuck you!" Gianna stepped forward.

"Ah ah." Emorie shook her head, leading the saw forward like a knight with a sword. "I wouldn't take another step unless you'd like to end up like your buddy over here." she laughed. "Believe me, after the colossal fuck up Darren turned out to be, I'm not making the same mistake as him!"

In a state of disbelief, Gianna was struggling with her next point of action.

"...Why did you do this, Emorie? Huh? Why? What the fuck

was the point!?" Gianna yelled.

"For justice."

"Justice?"

"Did I stutter, dumb whore?"

"Ex-fucking-scuse me?"

"The way all of you sick bastards idolized the she devil..." Emorie kicked Valeria's body. "As if SHE was some sort of CHEF!? HA! You assholes make me want to kill you!"

"Huh?"

"Aside from her promiscuity, as you can see." Emorie signaled to the photos on the floor. "This gutter rat was responsible for much, much worse. You see Gianna, Valeria over here STOLE each and every recipe from yours truly!" Emorie declared aggressively, with an eye twitch.

"She stole your recipe ideas?"

"Not my property." Emorie began. "That's the fucking excuse she'd use. Just because she found my notebook in my locker, she claimed that it was her restaurant, her property! BULLSHIT!" she screamed.

"Emorie, I didn-"

"You didn't know? Tch. Of course not! How could you when

you never bothered getting to know me? All of you pieces of shit treated me like I was Valeria's bitch, like I was some piece of communal chewing gum for all of you to chew and spit back out. A line of communication between the shit and the rat. And you know what? I fucking had it. All of you, so pathetic."

"So you're first fucking instinct is to kill everyone? What the fuck Emorie? You're sick!"

"Sick? No, no I'm simply a woman scorned one too many fucking times. What would you know? Huh? Reaching for the rope and making your way up the well, only to be pushed back fucking down by the hand offering to help you!"

"Why didn't you just leave?"

"And let her continue her bullshit with somebody else? Bitch please! I knew something had to be done, and that I was the only one MATURE enough to act. So I hatched a plan. A plan to burn down Val's. With her restaurant destroyed, she'd have nothing to leap to, a lost lamb ready for the slaughter. And to ensure bad press, I unfortunately had to kill Redmond Thatcher. With one of the biggest critics found dead, I wrongfully assumed the media would pin Valeria as responsible."

"But that didn't happen, Valeria was painted as a victim in all this." Gianna interrupted.

"The tears of a squealing pig are far more delicious to the masses than that of one already dead." Emorie scoffed. "Giving herself this bullshit narrative of being oh so heartbroken and remorseful - all a fucking act."

"And what about Darren, huh? What part does he play in all of this?"

"Oh Darren...a poor, dumb idiot." Emorie started. "I needed an accomplice, someone with as much hate for Valeria as myself." she shrugged. "The fool believed Valeria killed Redmond and was responsible for the fire. And after I sent him 'evidence' and 'motive', he agreed to the offer I presented to him. Ironic, really. The man came to Amber Creek to avenge Redmond, only to help his killer the entire time!" Emorie viciously laughed, before abruptly stopping. "After last year, I had to up the ante and craft a plan that would be sure to ruin Valeria. Alejandro would get the blackmail material from Marcellus, and then Darren and I would kill each and every one of you. Things were going alright, until *he* decided to blow shit up and kill Alejandro, and then you had to go and kill *him*! And then Marcellus had to get involved for some fucking reason and kill Valeria! Trying to kidnap *me* of all people? Tch." she paused. "He damn nearly ruined everything!"

"So then what was all this for? Nothing? Valeria's dead, Alejandro is dead, your reason for doing this is gone, so why not run? Leave town and never look back." Gianna suggested.

"I've already lost far too much already, I'm afraid. I have no choice but to see things through to the bitter end!" Emorie proclaimed. "You see, the one thing with him I failed to take into consideration was how narrow-minded he was. He loved Basil, you know that, right?"

"H-he did?" Gianna just continued to let Emorie speak, knowing her words wouldn't reach her.

"An eye for an eye. I killed his unrequited love, so he killed my requited love. Alejandro should still fucking be here, by my side, watching this shithole burn to the fucking ground." Emorie snapped. "He was supposed to..." her voice trailed off in despair. "Nevertheless, you did me a favor by killing that asshole."

"A favor, really?"

"Exactly! See, you *are* quick! And it's for that reason, my dear colleague, that I have decided to spare your life, but yours only."

"W-what!? Really?"

"No! Stupid bitch!" Emorie laughed, running towards Gianna with the saw.

"Girl fuck you!" Gianna insulted, jumping across a table to her side, narrowly missing Emorie's swing with the saw. Gianna stood back up, walking a few steps back as Emorie held the saw in her hands.

"You know, I was wondering why Valeria's food was so shit, and you answered my question for me! It was YOUR shitty recipe!" she snidely commented. "Nothing but a second-rate chef."

"You dumb bitch!" Emorie screamed in a fit of rage, jumping up on the table with the help of a chair and jumping down on Gianna, swinging down the saw. Gianna grabbed a chair from behind her and swung it against the saw, countering it, and falling back. "How DARE you! YOU of all people! Some talentless WHORE!"

"I'm." Gianna started huffing. "Not a whore!" She grabbed a

piece of the broken chair leg and stabbed Emorie in the leg. "ARGHHHH!" Emorie screamed. "I'm going to KILL you!" "Funny, I think Darren was thinking the same thing when I stabbed him too. And you know where that got him!" Gianna grinned, standing back up and running past Emorie, and standing where Emorie once stood.

"I knew I should've killed you first!" Emorie roared, revving the saw.

Gianna attempted to get out of the way, but her foot got caught between the pieces of Marcellus and the body of Valeria. "Fuck!" she screamed, with Emorie prepared to charge, similar to a lance.

***

Despite being fired, Pierre felt it would be a gesture of good faith to show up to the soft opening with well wishes for Gianna. Even though he had been fired hours prior, Pierre felt at peace, finally making a decision he could feel proud of. Looking at Val's parking lot, he noted that it must be a full house, and for that reason, he decided to enter from the back entrance. "They're probably in the dining room making final preparations." he assumed, as he went to quietly open the back door. "Can't let *her* know that I'm here." he took a deep breath. "Mr. Whitlock?" Harold questioned, standing in the alley by the trash cans. He threw something to the ground with haste before standing up right. "You shouldn't be here," he asserted, preventing Pierre from opening the door. "Your employment was terminated. You should quickly leave before she catches you."

"Harold Dunbar showing consideration? How the mighty have fallen!" Pierre teased, sniffing the air. "And is that...? Harold! You naughty boy! Smoking weed on the job!?"

"Silence! Tonight just happens to be very stressful for me. I don't need to hear it from you."

"Okay, okay! I won't say anything about that if you don't say anything about this" Pierre suggested. "I just wanted to wish Gianna some good luck before the opening. I haven't been the best person..."

"No need to state the obvious." Harold smirked. "Go on, say what you need to." he approved.

"Thanks, man. I really appreciate it." Pierre smiled with sincerity, getting ready to head inside.

"Hey." Harold interrupted once more. "Good on you, for standing up for yourself. You did what needed to be done. I'm proud of you, Pierre." Harold smiled, letting Pierre enter the kitchen. Pierre gave Harold a nod before heading inside, as though to give his respect.

Inside the restaurant, Pierre was greeted by the sound of Valeria and Gianna speaking loudly from the dining room. "As I thought." he whispered to himself, deciding to crouch to avoid being seen in the other room. Pierre jumped back after hearing the sounds of stomping coming from the locked walk in freezer. "Huh?" he asked, unlocking the door.
"G-get me out of here, please!" Heather pleaded, laying on the floor, shivering. "We need to leave!"
"What the hell?" Pierre almost screamed before catching himself and instead whispering. "Dude, what happened."

Heather slowly started to stand up, before groaning in pain.
"Pierre, you need to leave immediately and get the police." Heather said with urgency.
"What happened to you?"
"Valeria stabbed me and locked me in here! She's been hiding

quite a lot from everyone." Heather explained. "But we really need to leave! The Silhouette is here!"

"The who?"

"The Silhouette! The killer!"

"Well why didn't you just say that!"

"I- ugh! Never mind that, there's a bomb in the freezer!"

"A bomb!?"

Pierre looked into the freezer and saw a box with a timer on it counting down from "27:13", with wires sticking out from all ends of the box. "The hell is going on here?"

"Did Valeria do this?"

"No, it wouldn't make much sense. It would've been one thing if she burned down the original building, but to do it twice and proceed to kill her staff would be an illogical move on her part. This is the work of someone else. Quick, where is everybody!?" Heather asked,

"W-well, uh, Harold is outside not doing anything he shouldn't, and Valeria is talking to Gianna out in the dining room, but if she's out there, then Gianna is in danger!"

"It can't be..." Heather paused. "Pierre, Gianna will be fine for the moment, I need to speak with you and Harold outside immediately."

"But what about the bomb!?"

"It looks as if it were designed to demolish the building, and no more than that. The Silhouette must've crafted this alongside their modified saw." Heather confirmed. "This will only take a moment, quick!"

***

Heather felt like a complete idiot, missing the clues that had been in front of her the entire time. "Why would an up-and-coming chef demote herself to an assistant position?" she shook her head in frustration. "Unless she had something to prove, some unfinished business." she concluded.

Pierre and Heather snuck back outside, with Heather holding a frozen slab of meat against her wound.

"Pierre, oh my- Ms. Caine!?" Harold jumped, dropping his joint again. "What on earth is going on here?"

"Don't ask me, I'm in the dark as much as you are." Pierre shrugged.

"Darren wasn't the mastermind behind these killings, he was simply acting as a pawn for the true culprit!" Heather revealed.

"Do you mean Valeria, since she stabbed you and all?" Pierre questioned.

"Valeria did WHAT?" Harold gasped.

"No, I believe she was covering for someone else." Heather elaborated,

"But then for who?" Pierre questioned.

"There's only one possibility..." Heather started. "Someone who, despite having it all, still had a deep-seated grudge to settle."

"Ms. Wall- Emorie!? But there's no way-"

"*Emorie*!? That goodie two shoes? The girl doesn't even curse!" Pierre said in disbelief.

"I had initially ruled her out as a suspect myself, considering her relationship with Alejandro. But, what if she killed Basil for knowing about the Silhouette, and Darren killed Alejandro as revenge?" Heather suggested.

"What's a silhouette got to do with any of this?" Harold asked, puzzled.

"That's the name she gave the killer." Pierre answered.

"I see, but why would she be targeting all of us?" Harold questioned.

"To get back at Valeria." Heather responded. "This has all been for the sake of revenge, with Valeria being the main target and the lot of us just being fodder for her kill count."

"What did Valeria do?" Piere asked.

"She stole Emorie's recipes and claimed them as her own to boost her career into the spotlight. No wonder Emorie was able to reach such great heights in the year she was gone, she always had the gift within her." Heather finished.

"This is all too terrible to think about, surely you can't believe-"

Heather took out a voice recorder from her back pocket, and played the contents, which accounted for her discovery and the confrontation she had with Valeria.

"I found Emorie's recipe cards in Valeria's office. I believe Valeria tried to kill me to ensure the truth never came out."

"And if she was willing to kill you, what's stopping her from killing Gianna?" Pierre nervously asked. "What's to say Valeria doesn't just snap?

"I'm going back in there; I have to stop her." Heather asserted.

"And what about the bomb?" Pierre asked.

"A bomb? What do you mean? Why didn't you lead with that!?" Harold jumped.

"...I'll quickly take care of things and ensure everybody gets out safely."

"I cannot accept that." Harold shook his head.

"Neither can I." Pierre added. "Look, I know you might not know us that well, but we are just as involved with this mess as you are. You're in no state to head in, especially if Valeria and Emorie are inside.

"I agree, Ms. Caine. Leave this to us."

"No, I cannot allow anyone else to get hurt, I-"

"Nope. My mind is made up, I'm going in too. I need to save Gianna. You in, Harold?"

"I'm of the same opinion. We'll all make it out alive." Harold added. "I failed Basil...I won't fail Ms. McKnight as well." he nodded.

"Heh, you guys sure are a persistent bunch." Heather chuckled with respect. She grunted in pain from the stab wound. "It hurts like a bitch but luckily Valeria didn't hit anything too important, so I should be fine." Heather explained. "Let's go."

The timer now reads "18:07", counting down.

***

The sun began to set outside and the lighting in the restaurant grew darker. Gianna was stuck and her death was imminent.

"Fuck. Fuck. Fuck." she kept repeating over and over. "It can't end like this!" She struggled trying to get her foot freed but fell back onto the floor. "What the hell? It's like something's grabbing me!" she exclaimed.

"Time to do what Darren failed to finish!" Emorie smirked, running towards Gianna with the saw.

***

Something took hold of Pierre as he returned into the kitchen. From the second he heard the sounds of Gianna screaming in terror, and the sound of a motorized saw, Pierre, with disregard for his ankle, ran out into the dining room. At this point, nothing else mattered as he plunged himself in between Emorie's saw and Gianna, as the saw pierced his stomach, and he began coughing up blood. The saw blade got stuck in his stomach, as Emorie struggled to remove the weapon. More blood began pouring out of his mouth, as he moved Valeria's hand off of Gianna's ankle, freeing her. He smiled.

"P-Pierre? Why?" Gianna shook her head in disbelief.

"I'm sorry, Gigi." His smile grew larger as he fell to the floor. "This time, live for yourself." Pierre thought to himself as blood continued to clog his throat, leaving him unable to breathe. Pierre's vision went dark, and his hearing went out, with Gianna's screams and cries no longer being heard, as Pierre lay on the floor, dead.

***

"Gianna are you- Oh my god, no..." Heather stopped herself, as she entered the dining room from the kitchen with Harold.
"Pierre...Why did you...?" Harold shook his head in disbelief.
"Fuck YOU!" Emorie screamed, kicking Pierre's corpse. 'God FUCKING dammit! Again!?" she yelled in frustration.

Harold grabbed Gianna's arm and helped her back up, holding her behind him as he slowly backed up, away from Emorie, who was throwing a temper tantrum.
"Stupid fucking drunk, stupid fucking whore, stupid fucking-" she stopped, before turning her body towards the trio and away from the bodies on the floor. "You had to ruin everything, didn't you?"
"You did it yourself you fucking loser." Gianna mocked.
"Gianna, are you sure mocking her is a good idea?" Heather warned.
"I agree, we should be getting out of here now-" Harold began.

"None of you move for one fucking second." Emorie threatened, taking a detonator out from her pocket. "Did you seriously think that I'd wait for a fucking timer? I can blow this place to hell whenever I want! If any of you move, I'll end it all!"

As Emorie continued with her threats, she failed to notice Valeria standing back up, holding the knife Marcellus used to stab her.

"Now, I'm going to leave and when I do you'll all be-"

"Dead!" Valeria whispered in Emorie's ear as she gasped.

"There's no way-" Valeria slit Emorie's throat, and she fell to the floor, bleeding out.

Gianna jumped back in shock as Valeria cracked her neck and wiped the blood off of her knife.

"Now this is disappointing. Betrayed on every corner I fear." Valeria shrugged. "Oh well, I can always find new staff. Now, what to do with you three... And you! I could've sworn I killed you." She pointed the knife at Heather.

"You may copy however many recipes you want, but you can never match the original. I guess Emorie was just better than you in that sense!" Heather barked back. "Can't cook by yourself, and certainly can't kill either!"

"You're a real thorn in my side, you know that? The only regret I have through all this is bringing you to Amber Creek to begin with!"

"So you're the one who sent me the letter?"

"Guilty as charged." Valeria chuckled.

"But why?" Heather asked.

"Quite simple, really. I knew what Emorie was planning to do all along. I knew she planned on trying to destroy my reputation and so I planned ahead accordingly. I assumed that by having the legendary H.C Holmes snooping around, you could take out the trash for me. However, as with this runt," she pointed to Emorie. "You disappointed me."

"And the note telling me to leave?"

"Mine as well. Consider it...motivation." she laughed. "When I found out what Emorie was planning, truth be told, I thought that it would be the perfect cover!"

"What do you mean?" Harold asked.

"I was broke, Harold. I knew that by having my restaurant burn down, I would be able to collect the funds to pay off my debts. I played off the sympathy of those foolish enough to listen to my victim act and garnered enough funds from donors to begin anew. The icing on the cake was Redmond dying, now that was something that worked out way better than I could have imagined."

"Because of the bad review, huh?" Gianna added. "Emorie took care of the dirty work for you, without her even realizing it."

"It's crazy how the world works, isn't it? Though I have no room to complain." Valeria explained.

Harold stepped forward in hopes of empathizing with Valeria.

"Valeria, this isn't you!" he insisted. "As I would tell Basil..."

"Oh shut up old man!" Valeria denounced, ripping the saw off of Pierre's body, revving it up, and quickly decapitating Harold, the rest of his body falling to the floor as his head bounced like a deflating basketball.

"What the fuck!?" Gianna shrieked.

"I cannot leave any loose ends, unfortunately. If any of my staff survives, then, well, there won't be enough room for people to sympathize with me! A sole survivor of a mass killing has a much more beautiful ring to it than if everyone lived! Don't you think? At the end of the day, you're all just my pawns.

Now then, it's your turn!"

Before Valeria could kill Heather and Gianna, Emorie, with the last of her breath, pressed the detonator button, causing a combustion of flames from the walls and from the freezer and storage space in the kitchen. Gianna, Heather and Valeria were knocked back. A piece of the wall crushes the remains of Emorie, killing her.

***

There was a ringing in Gianna's ears as she rose up from the ground, covered in dirt and dust. The area around her was on fire and the glass ceiling above her began to crack. "Heather? Where are you?" she yelled out, standing up. Gianna could barely hear. As she walked through the remains of the dining room, the scent of flames consumed her senses. "Heather!" she screamed again. From behind Gianna, Valeria stood, holding a piece of concrete in her hand, creeping up. Gianna continued to call out for Heather, but with no luck. The glass ceiling was nearly about to shatter.

Despite not being able to hear or smell, Gianna could see the reflection from a piece of glass by her feet and saw that Valeria was preparing to knock her dead with the concrete.

"Now then..." Valeria began as she prepared to swing down on Gianna. "Let's end this!"

Gianna turned and fell to the floor, but before Valeria could kill her, the ceiling shattered, and large chunks of glass rained down like a violent storm. Valeria looked up as the glass fell, whereas Gianna scooted back to avoid any injury. Several large pieces of glass landed around Valeria, as she looked back at Gianna.

"Today's...not...your day..." she spoke, as she began to gush blood. "Ugh-" she choked, with large pieces of glass ticking out of her head, left eye, face, and back. She dropped the piece of concrete onto the ground. Valeria tried to take out the piece on the top of her head, shaking as she did so. The shard was longer than Valeria thought as the long, narrow piece of glass was thrown to the floor, and blood began squirting from the top of her head. Valeria continued to try and take the shards out as more blood began pouring from her body. Taking out a piece from her face, the glass ripped her skin off the bottom half of her face, leaving her flesh exposed. Gianna looked in horror as Valeria peeled off her own face. "W..e...ll t..h..en..." she stuttered, falling on her back dead, the glass shards sticking out piercing her and exiting through her stomach.

Gianna fell back, everything going black.

***

When Gianna woke up, her eyes were greeted by the clear sky, a sight that brought her comfort from the tribulations of the night. Sitting up, Gianna turned and saw Heather, who sat next to her. "Oh, good, you're up." Heather chuckled.
"What happened?" Gianna questioned, getting up. "Is it over?"
"It's over..." Heather sighed with relief. "You were only out for a little bit; I dragged you out here from the rubble."
"And Valeria?"
"She's...well... dead." Heather sighed. "And so are any chances of the truth of tonight being exposed.
"M-my pocket." Gianna signaled, as Heather reached in and grabbed a recorder.
"You did not-"
"An investigator is always prepared, isn't she?"
"Very good!" Heather smiled, before slouching back.

Gianna was unsure as to where she would go after this, with everything she knew being gone. "Pierre..." her voice trailed off. "I won't let your death be in vain." she asserted.

"How do you feel?" Heather asked.

"I think I'm feeling good." Gianna nodded. "You?"

"Y'know, aside from the stab wound, just peachy. I know that Eli will get a kick out of this" Heather chuckled.

Gianna took a huge sigh of relief as the sounds of ambulances and police sirens overtook the area. She was at peace, the stress that had overtaken Gianna over the course of the past week finally subsiding - the nightmare finally over.